LARGE PRINT ROB
Roberts, Nora.
Sullivan's woman

FEB 2 4 2004

Sullivan's Woman

NORA ROBERTS

Sullivan's Woman

THORNDIKE
CHIVERS

This Large Print edition is published by Thorndike Press®, Waterville, Maine USA and by BBC Audiobooks, Ltd, Bath, England.

Published in 2003 in the U.S. by arrangement with Harlequin Books, S.A.

Published in 2003 in the U.K. by arrangement with Harlequin Enterprises II, B.V.

U.S. Hardcover 0-7862-6086-6 (Romance)
U.K. Hardcover 0-7540-7761-6 (Chivers Large Print)
U.K. Softcover 0-7540-7762-4 (Camden Large Print)

The text of this Large Print edition is unabridged.
Other aspects of the book may vary from the original edition.

Set in 16 pt. Plantin by Ramona Watson.

Printed in the United States on permanent paper.

British Library Cataloguing-in-Publication Data available

Library of Congress Cataloging-in-Publication Data

Roberts, Nora.
    Sullivan's woman / Nora Roberts.
        p. cm.
    ISBN 0-7862-6086-6 (lg. print : hc : alk. paper)
    1. Large type books.   I. Title.
PS3568.O243S85 2003
    813′.54—dc22   2003065690

Sullivan's Woman

Chapter 1

Cassidy waited. Mrs. Sommerson tossed a third rejected dress into her arms.

"Simply won't do," the woman muttered and scowled at a midnight-blue linen. After a moment's consideration this, too, was dumped into the pile over Cassidy's arms. Valiantly Cassidy held on to her patience.

After three months as a sales clerk in The Best Boutique, she felt she'd learned patience, but it hadn't been easy. Dutifully she followed the solid bulk of Mrs. Sommerson to another display of dresses. After twenty-seven minutes of standing around like a clothes rack, Cassidy thought, shifting the weight on her arms, her hard-earned patience was sorely strained.

"I'll try these," Mrs. Sommerson finally announced and marched back to the changing room. Mumbling only a little, Cassidy began to replace unsuitable dresses.

She jammed a loose hairpin into her

scalp in irritation. Julia Wilson, The Best's owner, was a stickler for neatness. No hair was allowed to tumble over the shoulders of her clerks. Neat, orderly and unimaginative, Cassidy concluded, and wrinkled her nose at the midnight-blue linen. It was unfortunate that Cassidy was disorganized, imaginative, and not altogether neat. Her hair seemed to epitomize her personality. There were shades from delicate blond to rich brown melding into a tone like gold in an old painting. It was long and heavy and protested against the confines of pins by continuously slipping through them. Like Cassie herself, it was unruly and stubborn yet soft and fascinating.

It had been the appeal of Cassidy's slightly unconventional looks that had prompted her hiring. Experience had not been among her qualifications. Julia Wilson had recognized a potential advertisement for her merchandise and knew that Cassidy's long, supple body would set off the bold colors and styles of her more adventurous line. The face was undoubtedly a plus, too. Julia hadn't been certain it was a beautiful face, but she'd known it was striking. Cassidy's features were sharp and angular, undeniably aristocratic. Her brows arched over long, lidded eyes that seemed oversized in her narrow face and were a surprising violet.

Julia had seen Cassidy's face, figure and her well-pitched voice as references but had insisted on having her pin up her hair. With it down around her shoulders, it lent a distressingly wanton quality to the aristocratic features. She was pleased with Cassidy's youth, with her intelligence and with her energy. Soon after hiring her, however, Julia had discovered she was not as pliable as her age had suggested. She had, Julia felt, an unfortunate tendency to forget her place and become overly friendly with the customers. More than once, she'd come upon Cassidy as she asked customers impertinent questions or gave unwarranted advice. From time to time her smile suggested she was enjoying some private joke. And often, far too often, she daydreamed. Julia had begun to have serious doubts about Cassidy St. John's suitability.

After returning Mrs. Sommerson's rejected choices to their proper place, Cassidy took up her post by the changing room. From inside she could hear the faint rustle of materials. Idle, her mind did what it invariably did when given the opportunity. It drifted back to the manuscript that lay spread over her desk in her apartment. Waiting.

As far back as memory took her, writing had been her dream. For four years of college she had studied the craft seriously. At nineteen she'd been left without family and with little money. She had continued to work her way through college in various odd jobs while learning the discipline and art of her chosen profession. Between her education and employment, Cassidy had been left with meager snatches of free time. Even these had been set aside for work on her first novel.

To Cassidy writing was not a career but a vocation. Her entire life had been guided toward it, leaving her room for few other attachments. People fascinated her, but there were few with whom she was deeply involved. She wrote of complex relationships, but her knowledge of them came almost entirely secondhand. What gave her work quality and depth were her sharp talent for observation and her surprising depth of emotion. For the greater part of her life, her emotions had found their release in her work.

Now, a full year after graduation, she continued to take odd jobs to pay the rent. Her first manuscript worked its way from publishing house to publishing house while her second came slowly to life.

As Mrs. Sommerson opened the door of the changing room, Cassidy's mind was deep into the reworking of a dramatic scene. Seeing her standing with proper handmaidenly reserve, Mrs. Sommerson nodded approvingly. She preened ever so slightly.

"This should do nicely. Don't you agree?"

Mrs. Sommerson's choice was a flaming-red silk. The color, Cassidy noted, accented her florid complexion but was an attractively sharp contrast to her fluffy black mane of hair. The dress might have been more appropriate if Mrs. Sommerson had been a few pounds lighter, but Cassidy saw possibilities.

"You'll draw eyes, Mrs. Sommerson," she announced after a moment's deliberation. With the proper accessories, she decided, Mrs. Sommerson might very likely look regal. The silk, however, strained over her ample hips. A sterner girdle, Cassidy diagnosed, or a larger dress. "I think we have this in the next size," she murmured, thinking aloud.

"I beg your pardon?"

Preoccupied, Cassidy failed to note the

dangerous arch of Mrs. Sommerson's brows. "The next size," she repeated helpfully. "This one's a bit snug through the hips. The next size up should fit you perfectly."

"This is my size, young woman." Mrs. Sommerson's bosom lifted then fell. It was an awe-inspiring movement.

Deep into solving the accessory problem, Cassidy smiled and nodded. "A splashy gold necklace, I should think." She tapped her fingertip against her bottom lip. "Just let me find your size."

"This," Mrs. Sommerson stated in a tone that arrested Cassidy's full attention, "*is* my size." Indignation seethed in every syllable. Recognizing her mistake, Cassidy felt a sinking sensation in her stomach.

Whoops, she said silently then pulled her scattered wits together. Before she could begin soothing Mrs. Sommerson's ruffled ego, Julia stepped from behind her.

"A stunning choice, Mrs. Sommerson," she stated in her well-modulated contralto. With a noncommittal smile, she glanced from her customer to her clerk then back again. "Is there a problem?"

"This young woman . . ." Mrs. Sommerson heaved another deep breath. "Insists I've made a mistake in my size."

"Oh, no, ma'am," Cassidy protested, but subsided when Julia arched a penciled brow in her direction.

"I'm certain what Miss St. John meant to say was that this particular style is cut a bit oddly. The sizes simply do not run true."

I should've thought of that, Cassidy admitted to herself.

"Well." Mrs. Sommerson sniffed and eyed Cassidy with disapproval. "She might have said so, rather than suggesting that *I* was a larger size. Really, Julia." She turned back to the changing room. "You should train your staff better."

Cassidy's eyes kindled and grew dark at the tone. She watched the seams of the red silk protest against Mrs. Sommerson's generous posterior. The quick glare from Julia had her swallowing retorts.

"I'll fetch the dress myself, Mrs. Sommerson," Julia soothed, slipping her personable smile back into place. "I'm certain it will be perfect for you. Wait for me in my office, Cassidy," she added in an undertone before gliding off.

With a sinking heart, Cassidy watched Julia's retreat. She recognized the tone all too well. Three months, she mused, then sighed. Oh, well. With one backward glance at Mrs. Sommerson, she moved down the narrow hallway and into Julia's small, smartly decorated office.

She surveyed the square, windowless room, then chose a tiny, straight-backed, bronze cushioned chair. It was here, she remembered, I was hired. And it's here I'll be fired. She jammed another rebellious pin into place and scowled. In a few minutes she'll walk in, lift her left brow and sit behind her perfectly beautiful rosewood desk. She'll look at me a moment, gently clear her throat and begin.

"Cassidy, you're a lovely girl, but your heart isn't in your work."

"Mrs. Wilson," Cassidy imagined herself saying, "Mrs. Sommerson can't wear a size fourteen. I was —"

"Of course not," Cassidy pictured Julia interrupting her with a patient smile. "I wouldn't dream of selling her one, but" — here Cassidy envisioned Julia lifting up one slender, rose-tipped finger for emphasis — "we must allow her illusions *and* her vanity. Tact and diplomacy are essential for a salesperson, Cassidy. I'm afraid you've yet to fully develop these qualities. In a shop such as this" — Julia would fold her hand on the desk's surface — "I must be able to depend, without reservation, on my

14

staff. If this were the first incident, of course, I'd make allowances, but . . ." Here Cassidy imagined Julia would pause and give a small sigh. "Just last week you told Miss Teasdale the black crepe made her look like a mourner. This is not the way we sell our merchandise."

"No, Mrs. Wilson." Cassidy decided she would agree with an apologetic air. "But with Miss Teasdale's hair and her complexion —"

"Tact and diplomacy," Julia would reiterate with a lifted finger. "You might have suggested that a royal-blue would match her eyes or that a rose would set off her skin. The clientele must be pampered while the merchandise moves. Each woman who walks out the door should feel she has acquired something special."

"I understand that, Mrs. Wilson. I hate to see someone buy something unsuitable; that's why —"

"You have a good heart, Cassidy." Julia would smile maternally then drop the ax. "You simply have no talent for selling . . . at least, not the degree of talent I require. I shall, of course, pay you for the rest of the week and give you a good reference. You've been prompt and dependable. Perhaps you might try clerking in a department store."

Cassidy wrinkled her nose at this point in her scenario, then quickly smoothed her features as the door behind her opened. Julia closed it quietly then lifted her left brow and moved to sit behind her rosewood desk. She studied Cassidy a moment then gently cleared her throat.

"Cassidy, you're a lovely girl, but . . ."

Cassidy's shoulders lifted and fell with her sigh.

An hour later, unemployed, she wandered Fisherman's Wharf, enjoying its cheerful shabbiness, its traveling carnival atmosphere. She loved the cornucopia of scents and sound and color. Here there was always a crowd. Here there was life in ever-changing flavors. San Francisco was Cassidy's concept of a perfect city, but Fisherman's Wharf was the end of the rainbow. Make-believe and reality walked hand in hand.

She passed through the emporiums, poking idly through barrels of trinkets, fingering newly imported silk scarfs and soaking up the noise. But the bay drew her. She moved toward it at an easy, meandering pace as the afternoon gave way to evening. The scent of fish dominated the air. Beneath it were the aromas of onions and spice and humanity.

She listened to the vendors hawk their wares and watched as a crab was selected and boiled in a sidewalk cauldron. The wharf was rimmed with restaurants and crammed with stores. Without apology, its ambience was vaguely dilapidated and faintly tawdry. Cassidy adored it. It was old and friendly and content to be itself.

Nibbling on a hot pretzel, she moved through stalls of hanging Chinese turnips, fresh abalone and live crabs. Wisps of fog began to curl at her feet, and the sun sank lower. She was grateful for her plum-colored quilted jacket as the breeze swept in from the bay.

If nothing else, she thought ruefully, I acquired some nice clothes at a tidy discount. Cassidy frowned and took a generous bite of her pretzel. If it hadn't been for Mrs. Sommerson's hips, I'd still have a job. After all, I did have her best interests at heart. Annoyed, she pulled the pins from her hair then tossed them into a trash can as she passed. Her hair tumbled to her shoulders in long, loose curls. She breathed a sigh of relief.

Rats. She chewed her pretzel aggressively and headed for the watery front yard of

Fisherman's Wharf. I needed that job. I really needed that stupid job. Depression threatened as she walked the dock between lines of moored boats. She began a mental accounting of her finances. The rent was due the following week, and she needed another ream of typing paper. According to her shaky calculations, both of these necessities could be met if she didn't put too much emphasis on food for the next few days.

I won't be the first writer to have to tighten her belt in San Francisco, she decided. The four basic food groups are probably overrated anyway. With a shrug she finished off the pretzel. That could be my last full meal for some time. Grinning, she stuck her hands in her pockets and strolled to the rail at the edge of the dock.

Like a gray ghost, the fog rolled in over the bay. It crept closer to land, swallowing up the water along the way. It was thin tonight, full of patches, not the thick mass that often coated the bay and blinded the city. To the west the sun dipped into the sea and shot spears of flame over the rim of the water. Cassidy waited for the last flash of gold. Already her mood was lifting. She was a creature of hope and optimism, of faith and luck. She believed in destiny. It was, she felt, her destiny to write. The sale of articles and occasional short stories to magazines kept the dream alive. For four years of college her life had revolved around perfecting her craft. Jobs kept a roof over her head and meant nothing more. Dating had been permitted only when her schedule allowed and was kept casual. As yet, Cassidy had met no man who interested her seriously enough to make her veer from the straight path she had chosen. There were no curves in her scheme of things. No detours.

The loss of her current job distressed her only temporarily. Even as the evening sky darkened and the lights of the wharf fluttered on, her mood shifted. She was young and resilient.

Something would turn up, she decided as she leaned over the rail. Wavelets slapped gently against the hull of a fishing boat beside her. She had no need for a great deal of money; any job would do. Clerking in a department store might be just right. Perhaps something in home appliances. It would be difficult to step on anyone's vanity while selling a toaster. Pleased with the thought, Cassidy pushed worries out of her head and watched the fog tumble closer. Its fingers reached toward her.

There was a chill in the air now as the breeze picked up. She let it wash over her, tossing her hair and waking up her skin. The sounds and calls from the stands became remote, muffled by the mist. It was nearly dark. She heard a bird call out as it flew overhead and lifted her face to watch it. The first thin light of the moon fell over her. She smiled, dreaming a little. Abruptly she drew in her breath as a hand gripped her shoulder. Before she could make a sound, she'd been turned around and was staring up into a stranger's face.

He was tall, several inches taller than Cassidy, with a shock of black curls around a lean, raw-boned face. Her mind worked quickly to categorize the face, rejecting handsome in favor of dangerous. Perhaps it was her surprise and the creeping fog and darkening sky that caused the adjective to leap into her mind. But she thought, as she looked up at him, that his features were more in tune with the Barbary Coast than Fisherman's Wharf. His eyes were a deep, intense blue under black, winged brows, and his forehead was high under the falling black curls. His nose was long and straight, his mouth full, and his chin faintly cleft. It was a compelling, hard-hitting face with no softening features. He had a rangy build

20

accentuated by snug jeans and a black pullover. After her initial shock passed, Cassidy gripped her purse tight and squared her shoulders.

"I've only got ten dollars," she told him, keeping her chin fearlessly lifted. "And I need it at least as badly as you."

"Be quiet," he ordered shortly and narrowed his eyes. They were oddly intent on her face, searching, probing in a manner that made her shiver. When he cupped her chin in his hand, Cassidy's courage slipped away again. Without speaking, he turned her head from one side to the other, all the while studying her with absolute concentration. His eyes were hypnotic. She watched him, speechless, as his brows lowered in a frown. There was speculation in the look. She tried to jerk away.

"Be still, will you?" he demanded. His deep voice sounded annoyed, and his fingers were very firm.

Cassidy swallowed. "Now listen," she said with apparent calm. "I've a black belt in karate and will certainly break both your arms if you try to molest me." As she spoke she glanced past his shoulder and was dismayed to see the lights of the restaurants behind them had dimmed in the fog. They were alone. "I can break a two-by-four in half with my bare hand," she added when his expression failed to register terror and respect. She noted that the fingers on her chin were strong, and that despite his rangy build his shoulders were broad. "And I can scream very loudly," she continued. "You'd better go away."

"Perfect," he murmured and ran his thumb along her jawline. Cassidy's heart thudded with alarm. "Absolutely perfect. Yes, you'll do." All at once the intensity cleared from his eyes, and he smiled. The transformation was so rapid, so startling, Cassidy simply stared. "Why would you want to do that?"

"Do what?" Cassidy asked, astonished by his metamorphosis.

"Break a two-by-four in half with your bare hand."

"Do *what?*" Her own bogus claim was forgotten. Confused, she frowned at him. "Oh, well, it's — it's for practice, I suppose. You have to think right through the board, I believe, so that —" She stopped, realizing she was standing on a deserted dock in the fog holding an absurd conversation with a maniac who still had her chin in his hand. "You'd really better let me go and be on your way before I have to do something drastic."

"You're exactly what I've been looking for," he told her but made no attempt to act on her suggestion. She noted there was a slight cadence to his speech that suggested an ethnic background, but she did not pause to narrow the choices.

"Well, I'm sorry. I'm not interested. I have a husband who's a linebacker for the 49ers. He's six feet five, two hundred and sixty-three pounds and *very* jealous. He'll be along any minute. Now let me go and you can have the blasted ten dollars."

"What the devil are you babbling about?" His brows lowered again. With the fog swirling thinly at his back, he looked fierce. Abruptly, one black brow flew up to disappear beneath the careless curls. "Do you think I'm going to mug you?" A flash of irritation crossed his face. "My dear child, I've no designs on your ten dollars or on your honor. I'm going to paint you, not ravish you."

"Paint me?" Cassidy was intrigued. "Are you an artist? You don't look like one." She considered his dashing, buccaneer's features. "What sort of an artist are you?"

"An excellent one," he replied easily and tilted her face a tad higher. A splash of moonlight found it. "I'm famous, talented and temperamental." The charming smile was back in his face, and the cadence was Irish. Cassidy responded to both.

"I'm desperately impressed," she said. He was obviously a lunatic but an appealing one. She forgot to be afraid.

"Of course you are," he agreed and turned her head to left profile. "It's only to be expected." He freed her chin at last, but the tingle of his fingers remained on her skin. "I've a houseboat just outside the city. We'll go there and I can start sketching you tonight."

Cassidy's eyes lit with wary amusement. "Aren't you supposed to offer to show me sketches, or is this a variation on an old theme?" She no longer considered him dangerous, merely persistent.

He sighed, and she watched the quick annoyance flash over his face. "The woman has a one-track mind. Listen . . . what is your name?"

"Cassidy," she answered automatically. "Cassidy St. John."

"Oh, no, half-Irish, half-English. We'll have trouble there." He stuck his hands into his pockets. His eyes seemed determined to know every inch of her face. "Cassidy, I have no need for your ten dollars, and no plans to tamper with your virtue. What I want is your face. I've a

24

sketch pad and so forth on my houseboat."

"I wouldn't go on Michelangelo's boat if he handed me that line." Cassidy relaxed the grip on her purse and pushed her hair from her shoulders. Though he made a swift sound of exasperation, she grinned.

"All right." She sensed the impatience in his stance as he glanced behind him. "We'll get a cup of coffee in a well-lit, crowded restaurant. Will that suit you? If I try anything improper, you can break the table in half with your famous bare hand and draw attention."

Cassidy's lips trembled into a fresh grin. "I think I could agree to that." Before she could say anything else, he had her hand in his and was pulling her toward the cluster of restaurants. She felt an odd intimacy in the gesture along with a sense of his absolute control and determination. He was a man, she decided, who wouldn't take no for an answer. He walked quickly. She wondered if he were perpetually in a hurry. His stride was smooth, loose-limbed.

He pulled her into a small, rather dingy café and found a booth. The moment they were seated he again fixed her with his intent stare. His eyes, she noted, were even more blue than they had seemed in the dim light. Their color was intensified by his thick black lashes and bronze-toned skin. Cassidy met him stare for stare as she wondered what sort of man lived behind that incredible shade of blue. It was the waitress who broke her attention.

"What'll ya have?"

"Oh . . . coffee," she said when her companion made no move to speak or cease his staring. "Two coffees." When the waitress clomped away, Cassidy turned back to him. "Why do you stare at me like that?" she demanded. It annoyed her that her nerves responded to the look. "It's very rude," she pointed out. "And very distracting."

"The light's dreadful in here, but it's some improvement over the fog. Don't frown," he ordered. "It gives you a line right here." Before she could move he had lifted a finger and traced it down between her brows. "You have a remarkable face. I can't decide whether the eyes are an advantage or a drawback. One tends to disbelieve violet."

As Cassidy attempted to digest this, the waitress returned with their coffee. Glancing up, he plucked the pencil from her pocket and gave her one of his lightning smiles. "I need this for a few minutes. Drink your coffee. Relax," he directed with a careless gesture of his hand. "This won't hurt a bit."

Cassidy obeyed as he began to sketch on the paper placemat in front of him. "Do you have a job we'll need to work around or does your fictitious husband support you with his football prowess?"

"How do you know he's fictitious?" Cassidy countered and forced her eyes away from the planes of his face.

"The same way I know you'd have a great deal of trouble with a two-by-four." He continued to sketch. "Do you have a job?"

"I was fired this afternoon," she muttered into her coffee.

"That simplifies matters. Don't frown, I'm not a patient man. I'll pay you the standard sitting fee." He glanced up as Cassidy's brows lifted. "What I have in mind should take no more than two months, if all goes well. Don't look so shocked, Cassidy, my intentions were pure and honorable from the beginning. It was only your lurid imagination —"

"My imagination is not that lurid," she tossed back indignantly. She shifted in her seat as she felt her cheeks warm. "When people come looming up out of the fog and seizing other people —"

"Looming?" he interrupted and stopped sketching long enough to give her a dry look. "I don't believe I did any looming or seizing tonight."

"It seemed a great deal like looming and seizing from my perspective," she grumbled before she sipped her coffee. Her eyes dropped to the sketch he made. She set down the cup, her eyes widening with surprised admiration. "That's wonderful!"

In a few bold strokes he had captured her. She saw not just the shape of her own hair, but an expression she recognized as essentially her own. "It's really wonderful," she repeated as he began another sketch. "You really *are* talented. I thought you were bragging."

"I'm unflinchingly honest," he murmured as his borrowed pencil moved across the placemat.

Recognizing the quality of his work, Cassidy became more enthusiastic. Her mind raced ahead. Steady employment for two months would be a godsend. By the end of that time she should have heard from the publishing house that had her manuscript under consideration. Two months without having to sell toasters! She would have her evenings free to work on her new plot. The benefits began to mount and multiply. Destiny must have sent Mrs. Sommerson in search of a dress that afternoon.

"Do you really want me to sit for you?"

"You're precisely what I need." His manner suggested that the matter was already settled. The second sketch was nearly completed. His coffee cooled, untouched. "I want you to start in the morning. Nine should be early enough."

"Yes, but —"

"Keep your hair down, and don't pile on layers of makeup, you'll just have to wash it off. You might smudge up your eyes a bit, but little else."

"I haven't said I'd —"

"You'll need the address, I suppose," he continued, ignoring her protests. "Do you know the city well?"

"I was born here," she told him with a superior sniff. "But I —"

"Well then, you shouldn't have any trouble finding my studio." He scrawled an address on the bottom of the placemat. Abruptly he lifted his eyes and captured hers again.

They stared at each other amid the clatter of cutlery and chatter of voices. What Cassidy felt in that brief moment she could not define, but she knew she had never experienced it before. Then, as quickly as it had occurred, it passed. He rose, and she was left feeling as if she had run a very long race in a very short time.

"Nine o'clock," he said simply; then as an afterthought he dropped a bill on the table for the coffee. He left without another word.

Reaching over, Cassidy picked up the placemat with the sketches and the address. For a moment she studied her face as he had seen it. Was her chin really shaped that way? she wondered and lifted her thumb and finger to trace it. She remembered his hand holding it in precisely the same fashion. With a shrug she dropped her hand then carefully folded the placemat. It wouldn't do any harm to go to his studio in the morning, she decided as she slipped the paper into her purse. She could get a look at things and then make up her mind if she wanted to sit for him or not. If she had any doubts, all she had to do was say no and walk out. Cassidy remembered his careless dominance and frowned. All I have to do, she repeated to herself sternly, is to say no and walk out. With this thought she rose and strolled out of the café.

Chapter 2

The morning was brilliantly clear, with a warmth promising more before afternoon. Cassidy dressed casually, not certain what was *de rigueur* for a prospective artist's model. Jeans and a full-sleeved white blouse seemed appropriate. As instructed she had left her hair loose, and her makeup was light enough to appear nonexistent. She had yet to decide if she would sit for the strange, intriguing man she had met in the fog, but she was curious enough to keep the appointment.

With the address safely copied onto her own notepad and tucked in her purse, Cassidy grabbed a cable car that would take her downtown. The scribbled address had surprised her, as she had recognized the exclusiveness of the area. Somehow she'd expected her artist to have his studio near her own apartment in North Beach. There the atmosphere was informal and enduringly bohemian. Traditionally, clutches of writers and artists and musicians inhabited that section of the city and maintained its flavor. She wondered if perhaps he had a patron who had set him up in an expensive studio. He hadn't fit her conception of an artist. At least, she corrected herself, until she had seen his hands. They were, Cassidy recalled, perhaps the most beautiful hands she had ever seen, long and narrow with lean, tapering fingers. The bones had been close to the surface. Sensitive hands. And strong, she added, remembering the feel of his fingers on her skin.

His face remained clear in her mind, and she brooded over its image for several moments. Something about it tugged at a vague memory, but she couldn't bring her recollection into focus. It was a distinctive face, unique in its raw appeal. She thought if she were an artist, it would be a face she would be compelled to paint. There were good bones there and shadows and secrets, dominated by the terrifying blue of his eyes.

The trolley's bells clanged and snapped Cassidy out of her reverie. Stupid, she thought and lifted her face to the breeze. I didn't even get his name, and I'm obsessed with his face. He's supposed to be obsessed with mine, not the other way around. She jumped from the trolley and stepped onto the sidewalk. She scanned the street numbers looking for the address. I was right, she mused, about the quality of the neighborhood.

Still, like all of the city, it was a fascinating mixture of the exotic and the cosmopolitan, the romantic and the practical. San Francisco's dual personality was as prevalent here as it was in Chinatown or on Telegraph Hill. There remained a blending of the antique and the revolutionary. Cassidy could hear the clang of the old-fashioned trolley as she looked up at a radically new steel-and-glass skyscraper.

The day was fine and warm, and her body enjoyed it while her mind drifted back to the plot that sat on her desk at home. She brought her attention back to the present when she reached the number corresponding to the address in her purse. She stood frowning.

The Gallery. Cassidy scanned the number on the door for confirmation, and her frown deepened. She'd browsed through The Gallery only a few months before, and she remembered quite well when it had opened five years ago. Since its opening it had gained an enviable reputation as a showcase for the finest art in the country. A showing at The Gallery could make a fledgling artist's career or enhance that of a veteran. Collectors and connoisseurs were known to gather there to buy or to admire, to criticize or simply to be seen. Like much of the city it was a combination of the elegant and the unconventional. The architecture of the building was simple and unpretentious, while inside was a treasure trove of paintings and sculpture. Cassidy was also aware that one of The Gallery's biggest draws was its owner, Colin Sullivan. She searched her memory for what she had read of him, then began to put the bits and pieces into order.

An Irish immigrant, he had lived in America for more than fifteen years; his career had taken off when he had been barely twenty. Oil was his usual medium, and a unique use of shading and light his trademark. He had a reputation for impatience and brilliance. He would be just past thirty now and unmarried, though there had been several women linked romantically with him. There had been a princess once, and a prima ballerina. His paintings sold for exorbitant sums, and he rarely took commissions. He painted to please himself and painted well. As she stood in the warmth of the morning sunlight piecing together her tidbits of gossip and information, Cassidy recalled why the face of her artist had jarred a memory. She'd seen his picture in the newspaper when The Gallery had opened five years before. Colin Sullivan.

She let out a long breath then lifted her hands to either side of her head to push at her hair. Colin Sullivan wanted to paint her. He had once flatly refused to do a portrait of one of Hollywood's reigning queens, but he wanted to paint Cassidy St. John, an unemployed writer whose greatest triumph to date was a short story printed in a woman's magazine. All at once she remembered that she'd thought he'd been a mugger, that she had said absurd things to him, that she had told him with innocent audacity that his sketches were good. In annoyance and humiliation she chewed on her lip.

He might have introduced himself, she thought with a frown, instead of sneaking up behind me and grabbing me. I behaved quite naturally under the circumstances. I've nothing to be embarrassed about. Besides, she reminded herself, he told me to come. He's the one who arranged the entire thing. I'm only here to see if I want to take the job. Cassidy shifted her purse on her shoulder, wished briefly she had worn something more dignified or more exotic and moved to the front door of The Gallery. It was locked.

She pushed against the door again then concluded with a sigh that it was too early for The Gallery to be open. Perhaps there was a back entrance. He had spoken of a studio; surely it would have its own outside door. With this in mind Cassidy strolled around the side of the building and tried a side door, which refused to budge. Undaunted, she continued around the square brick building to its rear. When another door proved uncooperative, she turned her attention to a set of wooden steps leading to a second level.

Craning her neck, she squinted against the sun and scanned the ring of windows. The glass tossed back the light. If I were an artist with a studio, she reflected, it would definitely be up there. She began to climb the L-shaped staircase. The treads were open and steep. Faced with another door at the top, she started to test the knob, hesitated and opted to knock. Loudly. She glanced back over her shoulder and discovered the ground was surprisingly far below. A tiny sound of alarm escaped her when the door swung open.

"You're late," Colin stated with a frown of impatience and took her hand, pulling her inside before she could respond. Her senses were immediately assailed with the scents of turpentine and oils. He looked no less formidable in broad daylight than he had in the murky fog. In precisely the same manner he had employed the night before, he caught her chin in his hand.

"Mr. Sullivan . . ." Cassidy began, flustered.

"Ssh!" He tilted her head to the left, narrowed his eyes and stared. "Yes, it's even better in decent light. Come over here, I want some proper sketches."

"Mr. Sullivan," Cassidy tried again as he yanked her across a high, airy room lined with canvases and cluttered with equipment. "I'd like to know a little more about all this before I commit myself."

"Sit here," he commanded and pushed her down on a stool. "Don't slouch," he added as he turned away.

"Mr. Sullivan! Would you please listen to me?"

"Presently," he replied as he picked up a wide pad and a pencil. "For now be quiet."

Totally at a loss, Cassidy sighed gustily and folded her hands. It would be simpler, she decided, to let him get his sketches out of his system. She allowed her eyes to wander and search the room.

It was large, barnlike, with wide windows and a skylight that pleased her enormously. The expanses of glass let in all the available sunlight. The floor was wood and bare, except for splatters of paint, and the walls were a neutral cream. Unframed canvases were stacked helter-skelter, facing the walls. Easels were propped here and there, and a large table was scattered with paints and brushes and rags and bottles. There was a couch at the far end of the room, sitting there as if added in afterthought. Three wooden chairs were placed at odd intervals as if pushed aside by an impatient hand and left wherever they landed. There were two other stools, two inside doors and a large goosenecked high-intensity lamp.

"Look out the window," Colin ordered abruptly. "I want a profile."

She obeyed. The vague annoyance she felt slipped away as she spotted a sparrow building a nest in the crook of an oak. The bird moved busily, carrying wisps of this and that in her beak. Patient and tenacious, she swooped and searched and built, then swooped again. Her wings caught the sun. Enchanted, Cassidy watched her. A quiet smile touched her lips and warmed her eyes.

"What do you see?" Colin moved to her, and her absorption was so deep she neither jolted nor turned.

"That bird there." She pointed as the sparrow made another quick dive. "Look how determined she is to finish that nest.

The whole thing built from bits of string and grass and whatever other treasures sparrows find. We need bricks and concrete and prefabricated walls, but that little bird can build a perfectly adequate home out of next to nothing, without hands, without tools, without a union representative. Marvelous, don't you think?" Cassidy turned her head and smiled. He was closer than she had imagined, his face near hers in order for him to follow her line of vision. As she turned, he shifted his eyes from the window and caught hers. She felt a sudden jolt, as if she had stood too quickly and lost her inner balance.

"You might be even more perfect than I had originally thought," Colin said. He brushed her hair behind one shoulder.

She suddenly remembered her resolve to be businesslike. "Mr. Sullivan —"

"Colin," he interrupted. He continued to arrange her hair. "Or just Sullivan, if you like."

"Colin, then," she said patiently. "I had no idea who you were last night. It didn't occur to me until I was standing outside The Gallery." She shifted, faintly disturbed that he remained standing so close. "Of course, I'm flattered that you want to paint me, but I'd like to know what's expected of me, and —"

"You're expected to hold a pose for twenty minutes without fidgeting," he began while he pushed her hair forward again then back over her other shoulder. His fingers brushed Cassidy's neck and caused her to frown. He appeared not to notice. "You're expected to follow instructions and keep quiet unless I tell you otherwise. You're expected to be on time and not to babble about leaving early so you can meet your boyfriend."

"I was on time," Cassidy retorted and tossed her head so that his arrangement of her hair flew into confusion. "You didn't tell me to come to the back, and I wandered around until I found the right door."

"Bright, too," he said dryly. "Your eyes darken dramatically when your Irish is up. Who named you Cassidy?"

"It's my mother's family name," she said shortly. She opened her mouth to speak again.

"I knew some Cassidys in Ireland," he commented as he lifted her hands to examine them.

"I don't know any of my mother's family," Cassidy murmured, disconcerted by the feel of his hands on hers. "She died when I was born."

"I see." Colin turned her palms up. "Your hands are very narrow-boned. And your father?"

"His family was from Devon. He died four years ago. I don't see what this has to do with anything."

"It has to do with everything." He lifted his eyes from her hands but kept them in his. "You get your eyes and hair from your mother's family, and your skin and bone structure from your father's. It's a face of contradictions you have, Cassidy St. John, and precisely what I need. Your hair must have a dozen varying shades and it looks as though you've just taken your head from a pillow. You're wise not to attempt to discipline it. Your eyes go just past Celtic-blue into violet and add a touch of the exotic with the shape of them. They tend to dream. But your bones are all English aristocracy. Your mouth tips the balance again, promising a passion the cool British complexion denies. Pure skin, just a hint of rose under the ivory. You haven't walked through life without having to scale a few walls, yet there's a definite aura of the ingenue around you. The painting I want to do must have certain elements. I need very specific qualities in my model. You have them." He paused and inclined his head.

41

"Does that satisfy your curiosity?"

She was staring at him, transfixed, trying to see herself as he described. Did her heritage so heavily influence her looks? "I'm not at all certain that it does," Cassidy murmured. She sighed, then her eyes found him again. "But I'm vain enough to want Colin Sullivan to paint me and destitute enough to need the job." She smiled. "Shall I be immortal when you've finished? I've always wanted to be."

Colin laughed, and the sound was warm and free in the big room. He squeezed her hands, then surprisingly brought them to his lips. "You'll do me, Cass."

Cassidy's fumbling reply was interrupted as the studio door swung open.

"Colin, I need to —" The woman who swirled into the room halted abruptly and fixed sharp eyes on Cassidy. "Sorry," she said as her gaze drifted to their joined hands. "I didn't know you were occupied."

"No matter, Gail," Colin returned easily. "You know I lock the door when I'm working seriously. This is Cassidy St. John, who'll be sitting for me. Cassidy, Gail Kingsley, a very talented artist who manages The Gallery."

Gail Kingsley was striking. She was tall and thin as a reed with a long, triangular

42

face set off by a spiky cap of vivid red hair. Everything about her was vital and compelling. Her eyes were piercingly green and darkly accented, her mouth was wide and slashed in uncompromising scarlet. Gold hoops poked through the spikes of vibrant hair at her ears. Her dress was flowing, without definite line, a chaotic mix of greens washed over silk. The effect was bold and breathtaking. She moved forward, and her entire body seemed charged with nervous energy. Even her movements were quick and sharp, her eyes probing as they rested on Cassidy's face. There was something in the look that made Cassidy instantly uncomfortable. It was a purposeful intrusion while it remained completely impersonal.

"Good bones," Gail commented in a dismissing tone. "But the coloring's rather dull, don't you think?"

Cassidy spoke with annoyed directness. "We can't all be redheads."

"True enough," Colin said and, lifting a brow at Cassidy, turned to Gail. "What was it you needed? I want to get back to work."

There is a certain aura around people who have been intimate, Cassidy thought. It shows in a look, a gesture, a tone of voice. In the moment Gail's eyes left Cassidy to

43

meet Colin's, she knew they were, or had been, lovers. Cassidy felt a vague sense of disappointment. Uncomfortable, she tried vainly to pull her hands from Colin's. She received an absentminded frown.

"It's Higgin's *Portrait of a Girl.* We've been offered five thousand, but Higgin won't accept unless you approve. I'd like to have it firmed up today."

"Who made the offer?"

"Charles Dupres."

"Tell Higgin to take it. Dupres won't haggle and he's fair. Anything else?" There was a simple dismissal in the words. Cassidy watched Gail's eyes flare.

"Nothing that can't wait. I'll go give Higgin a call."

"Fine." Colin turned back to Cassidy before Gail was halfway across the room. He was frowning at her hair as he pushed it back from her face. Over his shoulder, Cassidy watched Gail's glance dart back when she reached the door. Gail shut it firmly behind her. Colin stepped away and scanned Cassidy from head to toe.

"It won't do," he announced and scowled. "It won't do at all."

Confused by his statement, shaken by what she had recognized in Gail's eyes, Cassidy stared at him then ran her fingers through her hair. "What won't?"

"That business you have on." He made a gesture with his hand, a quick flick of the wrist, which encompassed her blouse and jeans and sandals.

Cassidy looked down and ran her palms over her hips. "You didn't specify how I should dress, and in any case I hadn't decided to sit for you." She shrugged her shoulders, annoyed with herself for feeling compelled to justify her attire. "You might have given me some details instead of scrawling down the address and bounding off."

"I want something smooth and flowing; no waist, no interruptions." He ignored Cassidy's comments. "Ivory, not white. Something long and sleek." He took her waist in his hands, which threw her into speechless shock. "You haven't any hips to speak of, and the waist of a child. I want a high neck so we won't worry about the lack of cleavage."

Blushing furiously, Cassidy slipped down from the stool and pushed him away. "It's my body, you know. I don't care for your observations on it or your — your hands on it, either. My cleavage or the lack of it has nothing to do with you."

"Don't be a child," he said briskly and

set her back on the stool. "At the moment, your body only interests me artistically. If that changes, you'll know quickly enough."

"Now just a minute, Sullivan." Cassidy slipped off the stool again, tossing back her head as she prepared to put him neatly in his place.

"Spectacular." He grabbed a handful of her hair to keep her face lifted to his. "Temper becomes you, Cass, but it's not the mood I'm looking for. Another time, perhaps." The corners of his mouth lifted as his fingers moved to massage her neck. His smile settled lazily over his face, and though Cassidy suspected the calculation, it was no less effective. She was conscious of his fingers on her skin. The essential physicality of the sensation was novel and intrigued her into silence. This was something new to be explored. His voice lowered into a caress no less potent than the hand on her skin. The faint lilt of Ireland intensified. "It's an illusion I'm looking for, and a reality. A wish. Can you be a wish for me, Cass?"

In that moment, with her face inches from his, their bodies just touching, the warmth of his fingers on her skin, Cassidy felt she could be anything he asked. Nothing was impossible. This was where

46

his power over women lay, she realized: in the quick charm, the piratical features, the light hint of an old country in his speech. Added to this was an undiluted sexuality he turned on at will and an impatience in the set of his shoulders. She knew he was aware of his power and used it shamelessly. Even this was somehow attractive. She felt herself submitting to it, drawn toward it while her emotions overshadowed her intellect. She wondered what his mouth would feel like on hers, and if the kiss would be as exciting as she imagined. Would she lose or find herself? Would she simply experience? As a defense against her own thoughts, she placed her hands on his chest and pushed herself to safety.

"You're not an easy man, are you, Colin?" Cassidy took a deep breath to steady her limbs.

"Not a bit." There was careless agreement in his answer. She defined what flicked over his face as something between annoyance and curiosity. "How old are you, Cassidy?"

"Twenty-three," she answered, meeting his eyes levelly. "Why?"

He shrugged, stuck his hands in his pockets then paced the room. "I'll need to know all there is to know about you before

47

I'm done. What you are will creep into the portrait, and I'll have to work with it. I've got to find the blasted dress quickly; I want to start. The time's right." There was an urgency in his movements that contrasted sharply with the man who had seduced her with his voice only moments before. Who was Colin Sullivan? Cassidy wondered. Though she knew finding out would be dangerous, she felt compelled to learn.

"I think I know one that might do," she hazarded while his mood swirled around the room. "It's more oyster than ivory, actually, but it's simple and straight with a high neck. It's also horribly expensive. It's silk, you see —"

"Where is it?" Colin demanded and stopped his pacing directly in front of her. "Never mind," he continued even as she opened her mouth to tell him. "Let's go have a look."

He had her by the hand and had passed through the back door before she could say another word. Cassidy took care to go along peacefully down the stairs, not wishing to risk a broken neck. "Which way?" he demanded as he marched her to the front of the building.

"It's just a few blocks that way," she said and pointed to the left. "But Colin —" Before she could finish her thought, she was being piloted at full speed down the sidewalk. "Colin, I think you should know . . . Good grief, I should've worn my track shoes. Would you slow down?"

"You've got long legs," he told her and continued without slackening his pace. Making a brief sound of disgust, Cassidy trotted to keep up. "I think you should know the dress is in the shop I was fired from yesterday."

"A dress shop?" This appeared to interest him enough to slow him down while he glanced at her. With a gesture of absent familiarity, he tucked her hair behind her ear. "What were you doing working in a dress shop?"

Cassidy sent him a withering stare. "I was earning a living, Sullivan. Some of us are required to do so in order to eat."

"Don't be nasty, Cass," he advised mildly. "You're not a professional dress clerk."

"Which is precisely why I was fired." Amused by her own ineptitude, she grinned. "I'm also not a professional waitress, which is why I was fired from Jim's Bar and Grill. I objected to having certain parts of my anatomy pinched and dumped a bowl of coleslaw on a paying customer. I won't go into my brief career as a switchboard operator. It's a sad, pitiful story, and it's such a lovely day." She tossed back her head to smile at Colin and found him watching her.

"If you're not a professional clerk or waitress or switchboard operator, what are you, Cass?"

"A struggling writer who seems singularly inept at holding a proper job since college."

"A writer." He nodded as he looked down at her. "What do you write?"

"Unpublished novels," she told him and smiled again. "And an occasional article on the effects of perfume on the modern man. I have to keep my hand in."

"And are you any good?" Colin skirted another pedestrian without taking his eyes from Cassidy.

"I'm positively brimming with fresh, undiscovered talent." She tossed her hair behind her shoulders then pointed. "There we are, The Best Boutique. I wonder what Julia will have to say about this. She'll probably think you're keeping me." She bit her lip to suppress a giggle then slid her glance back to his. "Have you any smoldering looks up your sleeve, Colin?" Mischief danced in her eyes as she paused outside the front door of the shop. "You could send me a few and give Julia something to talk about for weeks." She swung through the door, her lovely face flushed with laughter.

True to form, Julia greeted Colin with scrupulous politeness and only the faintest glimmer of curiosity. There was a speculative glance for her former clerk, then recognition of Colin widened her eyes. She lifted a brow at Cassidy's request for the oyster silk dress then proceeded to wait on them personally.

In the changing room Cassidy stripped off her jeans and marveled at the irony of life. Little more than twenty-four hours before, she had been standing outside that very room with discarded dresses heaped over her arms . . . without a thought of Colin Sullivan in her head. Now he seemed to dominate both her thoughts and her actions. The thin, cool silk was slipping over her head because he wished it. Her heart beat just a fraction quicker because he waited to see the results. Cassidy fastened the zipper, held her breath and turned. Her reflection stared back at her with undisguised awe.

The dress fell from a severely high neck in a straight line, softened by the fragility of the material. Her arms and shoulders gleamed under the thin transparency of its full sleeves. Her hair glowed with life against the delicacy of color. Cassidy let out her breath slowly. It was a wish of a dress, as romantic as the material, as practical as its line. In it she not only looked both elegant and vulnerable but felt it. With taut nerves she moistened her lips and stepped from the changing room.

Colin was charming Julia into blushes. The incongruity of flirtatious color in the cool, composed face turned Cassidy's nerves into amusement. There was the devil of a smile in Colin's eyes as he lifted Julia's hand and brushed his lips over her knuckles. Cassidy schooled her features to sobriety. A hint of a smile lurked on her lips.

"Colin."

He turned as she called his name. The smile that lit his face and brightened his eyes faded then died. Releasing Julia's hand, he took a few steps closer but kept half the room between them. Cassidy, who had been about to grin and spin a circle for inspection, stood still, hypnotized by his eyes.

Very slowly, his eyes left her face to travel down the length of her then back again. Cassidy's cheeks grew warm with the flurry of her emotions. How could he make her feel so vitalized then so enervated with just a look? She wanted to speak, to break her own trance, but the words were jumbled and uncooperative. She found she could only repeat his name.

"Colin?" There was the faintest hint of invitation in the word, a question even she did not understand.

Something flashed in his eyes and was gone. The intense concentration was inexplicably replaced by irritation. When he spoke it was brisk and dismissive.

"That will do very well. Have it packed up and bring it with you tomorrow. We'll start then."

Cassidy's mind raced with a hundred questions and a hundred demands. His tone stiffened her pride, however, and hers was cool when she spoke. "Is that all?"

"That's all." Temper hovered in his voice. "Nine o'clock tomorrow. Don't be late."

Cassidy took a deep breath and let it out carefully. In that moment she was certain she despised him. They watched each other for another minute while the air crackled with tension and something more volatile. Then she turned her back on him and glided into the changing room.

Chapter 3

Cassidy spent most of the night lecturing herself. By morning she felt she had herself firmly in hand. There had been absolutely no reason for her to be annoyed with Colin. His brisk, impersonal attitude over the dress was only to be expected. As she rode the trolley across town, she shifted the dress box into her other arm and determined to preserve a cool, professional distance from him.

He's simply my employer. He's an artist, obviously a temperamental one. She added the modifier with a sniff. Deftly she jumped from the cable car to finish the trip on foot. He's a man who sees something in my face he wants to paint. He has no personal feelings for me, nor I for him. How could I? I barely know Colin Sullivan. What I felt yesterday was simply the overflow of his personality. It's very strong, very magnetic. I only imagined that there was an immediate affinity between us. Things don't happen that way, not that fast. All there is between us is the bond between artist and subject. I was writing scenes again.

Cassidy paused at the base of the stairs that led to Colin's studio. Still, he might have thanked me for finding the dress he was looking for, she thought. Never mind. She made an involuntary gesture with her hand as she climbed the steps. He's so self-absorbed he probably forgot I suggested the shop in the first place. With a quick toss of her head, Cassidy knocked, prepared to be brisk and professional in her new employ. Her resolve wavered a bit when Gail Kingsley opened the door.

"Hello," she said and smiled despite the cool assessment in Gail's eyes. For an answer Gail made a sweeping arm gesture into the room that would have seemed overdone on anyone else. Flamboyance suited her.

Gail was just as striking today in a shocking-pink jumpsuit no other redhead would have had the courage to wear. Colin was nowhere in sight. Cassidy was torn between admiration for the redhead's style and disappointment that Colin hadn't answered the door. She felt juvenile and ragged in jeans and a pullover.

"Am I too early?"

Gail placed her hands on her narrow

hips and walked around Cassidy slowly. "No, Colin's tied up. He'll be along. Is that curl in your hair natural or have you a perm?"

"It's natural," Cassidy replied evenly.

"And the color?"

"Mine, too." Gail's bold perfume dominated the scents of paint. When she came back to stand in front of her, Cassidy met her eyes levelly. "Why?"

"Just curious, dear heart. Just curious." Gail flashed a quick, dazzling smile that snapped on and off like a light. It was momentarily blinding, then all trace of it vanished. "Colin's quite taken with your face. He seems to be drifting into a romantic period. I've always avoided that sort of technique." She narrowed her eyes until she seemed to be examining the pores of Cassidy's skin.

"Want to count my teeth?" Cassidy invited.

"Don't be snide." Gail touched a scarlet-tipped finger to her lips. "Colin and I often share models. I want to see if I can use you for anything."

"I'm not a box lunch, Miss Kingsley," retorted Cassidy with feeling. "I don't care to be shared."

"A good model should be flexible," Gail

reproved, stretching her slender arms to the ceiling in one long, luxurious movement. "I hope you don't make a fool of yourself the way the last one did."

"The last one?" Cassidy responded then immediately wanted to bite off her tongue.

"She fell desperately in love with Colin." Gail gave her quick light-switch smile again. Her sharp, rapid gestures skittered down Cassidy's nerves. She was a cat looking for something to stalk. "Worse, she imagined Colin was in love with her. It was really quite pathetic. A lovely little thing — milky skin, dark gypsy eyes. Naturally Colin was beastly to her in the end. He tends to be when someone tries to pin him down. There's nothing worse than having someone mooning and sighing over you, is there?"

"I wouldn't know," Cassidy returned in mild tones. "But you needn't worry that I'll be mooning and sighing over Colin. He needs my face, I need a job." She paused a moment. Perhaps, she thought, it's best to be clear from the start. "You won't have any trouble from me, Gail. I'm too busy to orchestrate a romance with Colin."

Gail stopped her pacing long enough to fix her with a speculative frown. The frown vanished, and she moved swiftly to the door. "That simplifies matters, doesn't it? You can change through there." She flung out an arm to her left and was gone.

Cassidy took time to inhale deeply. She shook her head. Artists, she decided, were all as mad as hatters. Shrugging off Gail's behavior, she moved to the door indicated and found a small dressing room. Closeting herself inside, Cassidy began to change. As before, the gown made her feel different. Perhaps, she thought as she pulled a brush through her hair, it's the sensation of real silk against my skin, or the elegant simplicity of the line and color. Or is it because it's the image of what Colin wants me to be?

Whatever the reason, Cassidy couldn't deny that she felt heightened when she wore the gown — more alive, more aware, more a woman. After giving herself one last quick glance in the mirror, she opened the door and stepped into the studio.

"Oh, you're here," she said foolishly when she saw Colin scowling at a blank canvas. She had only a side view of him, and he didn't turn at her entrance. His hands were stuffed in his pockets, and his weight was distributed evenly on both legs. There was an impression of sharp vitality held in check — waiting, straining a bit for

58

release. He was dressed casually, as she was now accustomed to seeing him, and the clothes seemed to suit his rangy, loose-limbed build. His face was in a black study: brows lowered, eyes narrowed, mouth unsmiling. The thought crossed Cassidy's mind that he was unscrupulously attractive and would be a terrifying man to care for. She remained where she was, certain he had not even heard her speak.

"I'm going to start on canvas straight away," he said. Still he did not turn to acknowledge her. "There're violets on the table." With one shoulder he made a vague gesture. "They match your eyes."

Cassidy looked over and saw the small nosegay tossed amid the artistic rubble. Her face lit with instant pleasure. "Oh, they're lovely!" Moving to the table, she took them then buried her face in their delicate petals. The fragrance was subtle and sweet. Touched and charmed, Cassidy lifted her smile to thank him.

"I want a spot of color against the dress," Colin murmured. His preoccupation was obvious and complete. He did not glance at her or change expression.

Pleasure shattered, Cassidy stared down at the tiny flowers and sighed. It's my fault, she thought ruefully. He bought them for the painting, not for me. It was ridiculous to think otherwise. Why in the world should he buy me flowers? With a shake of her head and a wry smile, she moved over to join him. "Do you see me there already?" she asked. "On the empty canvas?"

He turned then and looked at her, but the frown of his concentration remained. He lifted the hand that held the flowers. "Yes, they'll do. Stand over here, I want the light from this window."

As he propelled her across the room, Cassidy twisted her head to look up at him. "Good morning, Colin," she said in the bright, cheerful voice of a kindergarten instructor.

He lifted a brow as he stopped by the window. "Manners are the least of my concerns when I'm working."

"I'm awfully glad you cleared that up," Cassidy replied, smiling broadly.

"I've also been known to devour young, smart-tongued wenches for breakfast."

"Wenches!" Cassidy's smile became a delighted grin. "How wonderfully anachronistic. It sounds lovely when you say it, too. I do wish you'd said lusty young wenches, though. I've always loved that phrase."

"The description doesn't fit you." Colin lifted her chin with one finger and brushed her hair over her shoulder with his other hand.

"Oh." Cassidy felt vaguely insulted.

"Once I've set the pose, don't fidget. I just might throw an easel at you if you do." While he spoke, he moved her face and body with his hands. His touch was as impersonal as a physician's. I might as well be a still-life arrangement, Cassidy thought. By his eyes, she saw that his mind had gone beyond her and into his art. She recognized his expression of absolute concentration from her own work. She, too, had a tendency to block out her surroundings and step into her own mind.

At length he stood back and studied her in silence. It was a natural pose and simple. She stood straight, with the nosegay cupped in both hands and held just below her right hip. Her arms were relaxed, barely bent at the elbows. He had left her hair tumbled free, without design, over both shoulders. "Lift your chin a fraction higher." He held up a hand to stop the movement. "There. Be still and don't talk until I tell you."

Cassidy obeyed, moving only her eyes to watch him as he strode behind the easel again. He lifted a piece of charcoal. Minutes passed in utter silence as she watched the movements of his arms and shoulders and felt the probing power of his eyes. They returned again and again to her face. She knew he could look into her eyes and see directly into her soul, learning more perhaps than she knew herself. The sensation made her not nervous so much as curious. What would he see? How would he express it?

"All right," Colin said abruptly. "You can talk for the moment, but don't move the pose. Tell me about those unpublished novels of yours."

He continued to work with such obsessed concentration that Cassidy assumed he had invited her to talk only to keep her relaxed. She doubted seriously if her words made more than a surface impression. If he heard them at all, he would forget them moments later.

"There's only one actually, or one and a half. I'm working on a second novel while the first bounces from rejection slip to rejection slip." She started to shrug but caught herself in time. "It's about a woman's coming of age, the choices she makes, the mistakes. It's rather sentimental, I suppose. I like to think she makes the right choices in the end. Do you know it's very difficult to talk without your hands? I had no idea mine were so necessary to my vocabulary."

"It's your Gaelic blood." Colin frowned deeply at the canvas then lifted his eyes to hers. By the movement of his shoulders she knew he continued to work. "Will you let me read your manuscript?"

Surprised, Cassidy stared a moment before gathering her wits. "Well, yes, if you'd like. I —"

"Good," he interrupted and slashed another line on the canvas. "Bring it with you tomorrow. Be quiet now," he commanded before Cassidy could speak again. "I'm going to work the face."

Silence reigned until he put down the charcoal and shook his head. "It's not right." He scowled at Cassidy then paced. Unsure, she held the pose and her tongue. "You're not giving me the right mood. Do you know what I want?" he demanded. There was impatience and a hint of temper in his voice. She opened her mouth then closed it again, seeing the question had been rhetorical. "I want more than an illusion. I want passion. You've passion in you, Cassidy, more, by heaven, than I need for this painting." He turned to face her again, and she felt the room vibrate with his tension. Her heart began to quicken in response. "I want a promise. I want a woman who invites a lover. I want expectation and the freshness that springs from innocence. Untouched but not untouchable. It's that you have to give me. That's the essence of it." In his frustration, the cadence of his native land became more obvious. The fire of his talent flickered in his eyes. Fascinated, Cassidy watched him, not speaking even when he stopped directly in front of her. "There would be a softness in your eyes and just a trace of heat. There would be a giving in the set of your mouth that comes from having just been kissed, from waiting to be kissed again. Like this."

His mouth took hers quickly, stunningly. He framed her face with his hands, thumbs brushing her cheeks while he took the kiss into trembling intimacy with terrifying speed. His lips were warm and soft and experienced. His tongue plundered without warning. Somewhere deep within her came an answer. Passion, long overlooked, smoldered then kindled then licked tentatively into flame. She tasted the flavor of power. As quickly as his mouth had taken, it liberated.

Though she was unaware of it, her expression was exactly what he'd demanded of her — expectant, inviting, innocent.

Fleetingly he dropped his gaze to her mouth; then, taking his time, he removed his hands from her face. Impatience flickered in his eyes before he turned and strode to his easel.

Cassidy tried to steady her spinning brain. Reason told her the kiss had meant nothing, a means to an end, but her heart thudded in contradiction. In a few brief seconds he had stirred up a hunger she hadn't been aware of having, had stirred up desires she hadn't been aware she had. It was more a revelation, she thought bemusedly, than a kiss. Forcing her breathing to slow, she tried to keep the quick encounter in perspective.

She was a grown woman. Kisses were more common than handshakes. It was her treacherous imagination that had turned it into something else. *Only my imagination,* she decided as she calmed, and his utter effrontery. He'd taken her totally by surprise. He'd kissed her when he'd had no right to do so, and in a way that had been both proprietary and intimate. No man had ever been permitted either of the privileges, and his seizure of them had left her shaken. Cassidy could justify her reaction to Colin by intellectually dissecting the scene, its cause and results. She turned her emotions over to her mind and plotted the scene. She examined motivations. Still, something lingered inside her that could not quite be rationalized or explained away. Disturbed, she tried to ignore it.

"We'll stop now," Colin stated abruptly and put aside the charcoal. He glanced up as he cleaned his hands on a paint rag. She thought perhaps he saw Cassidy St. John again for the first time since he had set the pose. "Relax."

When Cassidy obeyed, she was surprised to find her muscles stiff. "How long have I been standing there?" she demanded as she arched her back. "A good bit more than twenty minutes."

Colin shrugged, his eyes back on the canvas. "Perhaps. It's moving nicely. Do you want coffee?"

Cassidy scowled at his casual dismissal of the time. "Twenty minutes is quite long enough to stand in one position. I'll bring a kitchen timer with me from now on, and yes, I want coffee."

He ignored the first two-thirds of her statement and headed for the door. "I'll fix some."

"Am I allowed to look?" She gestured toward the canvas as he drew back the bolt.

"No."

She made a sound of disgust. "What

about the others?" Her gesture took in the canvases against the wall. "Are they a secret, too?"

"Help yourself. Just stay away from the one I'm working on." Colin disappeared, presumably to fetch the promised coffee.

Making a face at the empty doorway, Cassidy set down the nosegay and wandered toward the neglected canvases. They were stacked here and tilted there, without order or design. Some were small while others were large enough to require some effort on her part to turn them around. Within moments, whatever minor irritation she'd felt was eclipsed by admiration for his talent. She saw why Colin Sullivan was considered a master of color and light. Moreover she saw the sensitivity she had detected in his hands and the strength she had felt there. There was insight and honesty in his portraits, vitality in his city scenes and landscapes. A play of shadows, a splatter of light, and the paintings breathed his mood. She wondered if he painted what he saw or what he felt, then understood it was a marriage of both. She decided that he saw more than the average mortal was entitled to see. His gift was as much in his perception as in his hands. The paintings moved her almost as deeply as the man had.

Carefully she turned another canvas. The subject was beautiful. The woman's undraped body lounged negligently on the couch that now sat empty at the far end of the studio. There was a lazy smile on her face and a careless confidence in the attitude of her naked limbs. From the milky skin and gypsy eyes, Cassidy recognized the model Gail had spoken of that morning.

"A lovely creature, isn't she?" Colin asked from behind. Cassidy started.

"Yes." She turned and accepted the proffered mug. "I've never seen a more beautiful woman."

Colin's brow arched as he moved his shoulders. "Of a type, she's nearly perfect, and her body is exquisite."

Cassidy frowned into her coffee and tried to pretend the stab of irritation didn't exist.

"She has a basic sexuality and is comfortable with it."

"Yes." Sipping her coffee, Cassidy spoke mildly. "You've captured it remarkably well."

Her tone betrayed her. Colin grinned. "Ah, Cass, it's an open book you are and surely the most delightful creature I've met in years." The thickened brogue rolled easily off his tongue. Better women than she, Cassidy was certain, had fallen for the Gaelic charm.

She tossed her head, but the glare she had intended to flash at him turned of its own volition into a smile. "I can't keep up with you, Sullivan." She studied him over the rim of her mug. Sunlight shot through her hair and shadowed the silk of the dress. "Why did you settle in San Francisco?" she asked.

Colin straddled one of the abandoned wooden chairs, keeping his eyes on her. She wondered if he saw her as a person now or still as a subject. "It's a cross section of the world. I like the contrasts and its sordid history."

"And that it trades on that sordid history rather than apologizing for it," Cassidy concluded with an agreeing nod. "But don't you miss Ireland?"

"I go back now and then." He lifted his coffee and drank deeply. "It feeds me, like a mother's breast. Here I find passion, there I find peace. The soul requires both." He glanced up at her again and searched her face. The violet of her eyes had darkened. Her expression revealed her thoughts. They were all on him. Colin turned away from the innocent candor of her eyes. "Finish your coffee. I want to perfect the preliminary outline today. I'll start in oil tomorrow."

The morning passed almost completely in silence while she took advantage of Colin's absorption to study him. She had read of the dark devil looks and fiery blue eyes of the volatile black Irish, and now she found them even more compelling in the flesh. She wondered at the strange quirk in her own personality that caused her to find moodiness appealing.

With only the barest effort she could feel the swift excitement of his lips on hers. Warmed, she drifted with the sensation. For a moment she imagined what it would be like to be held by him in earnest. Though her experience with men had been limited, her instincts told her Colin Sullivan was dangerous. He interested her too much. His dominance challenged her, his physicality attracted her, his moodiness intrigued her.

Gail Kingsley's scathing comment about Cassidy's predecessor came back to her. She had a quick mental picture of the red-head's demanding beauty and the model's sultry allure. Cassidy St. John, she mused, is at neither end of the spectrum. She isn't strikingly vivid nor steamily sexy. Feminine extremes apparently appeal to Colin both as an artist and as a man. She caught herself, annoyed with the train of her own thoughts. It would not do to get involved or form any personal attachments with a man like Colin Sullivan. Don't get too close, she cautioned herself. Don't open any doors. *Don't get hurt.* The last warning came from nowhere and surprised her.

"Relax."

Cassidy focused on Colin and found him staring down at the canvas. His attention was concentrated on what only he could see. "Go change," he directed without glancing up. Cassidy's thoughts darkened at his tone. Rude, she decided, was a mild sort of word for describing Sullivan the artist. Controlling her temper, Cassidy went back to the dressing room.

My worries are groundless, she told herself and closed the door smartly. No one could possibly get close enough to that man to be hurt.

A few moments later Cassidy emerged from the dressing room in her own clothes. Colin stood, facing the window, his hands jammed into his pockets, his eyes narrowed on some view of his own.

71

"I've left the dress hanging in the other room," Cassidy said coldly. "I'll just be off, since you seem to be done." She snatched up her purse from the chair. Even as she swung it over her shoulder and turned for the door, Colin took her hand in his.

"You've that line between your brows again, Cass." He lifted a finger to trace it. "Smooth it out and I'll buy you some lunch before you go."

The line deepened. "Don't use that patronizing tone on me, Sullivan. I'm not an empty-headed art groupie to be patted and babied into smiles."

His brow lifted a fraction. "Quite right. Then again, there's no need to go off in a tiff."

"I'm not in a tiff," Cassidy insisted as she tried to jerk out of his hold. "I'm simply having a perfectly normal reaction to rudeness. Let go of my hand."

"When I'm through with it," he replied evenly. "You should mind your temper, Cass my love. It does alluring things to your face, and I'm not one for resisting what appeals to me."

"It's abundantly clear the only appeal I have for you is on that canvas over there." Cassidy wriggled her hand in an attempt to free it. With a quick flick of the wrist,

Colin tumbled her into his chest. Mutinous and glowing, her face lifted to his. "Just what do you think you're doing?"

"You challenge me to prove you wrong." There was amusement in his eyes now and something else that made her heart beat erratically.

"I don't challenge you to anything," she corrected with a furious toss of her head. Her hair swung and lifted with the movement then settled into its own appealing disarray.

"Oh, but you do." His free hand tangled in her hair and found the base of her neck. "You threw down the gauntlet the night I found you in the fog. I think it's time I picked it up."

"You're being ridiculous." Cassidy spoke quickly. She realized her temper had carried her into territory she would have been wise to avoid. As she began to speak again, he caught her bottom lip between his teeth. The movement was sudden, the pressure light, the effect devastating.

Though she made a tiny sound of confused protest, her fingers clutched at his shirt instead of pushing him away. The tip of his tongue traced her lip as if experimenting with its flavor. When he released it, she stood still. Her eyes locked with his.

"This time when I kiss you, Cass, it's to pleasure myself," he said as his mouth lowered to take hers. Knowing he would meet no resistance, he circled her waist to mold her against him. Cassidy responded as if she'd been waiting for the moment all of her life. Her body seemed to know his already and fitted its soft, subtle curves to his firm, taut lines. Her hands traveled from his neck to tangle in his hair, while her mouth grew more mobile under his. For one brief instant, he crushed her to him with staggering force, ravishing her conquered mouth. Just as swiftly, her lips were freed. Her breath came out in a quick rush as she gripped him for balance. He held her close, keeping their bodies as one, his eyes boring into hers. Only the sound of their mixed breathing disturbed the silence.

The weakness Cassidy felt was a shock to her. Her knees trembled beneath her and she shook her head in a quick attempt to deny what he had awakened. Something deep and secret was struggling for release. The strength of it alarmed and fascinated her. Still, her fear outweighed her curiosity. Instinct warned her it was not yet time. Even as she found the will to draw away, Colin pulled her closer.

"No, Colin, I can't." She swallowed as

her hands pushed against his chest. She watched his eyes darken as his lips lingered just over hers.

"I can," he murmured, then crushed her mouth. She swirled back into the storm.

Nothing in her experience had ever prepared her for the new demands of her own body. With innocent allure, she moaned against his mouth. She felt his lips move against hers as he murmured something. Then he plundered, pulling her down into a world of heat and darkness. A quickening fear rose with her passion. When he released her mouth, her breath came in short gasps. Her eyes clouded with desire and confusion.

"Please, Colin, let me go. I think I'm frightened."

He was capable of taking her, she knew, and of making her glad that he had. His eyes were blazing blue, and she kept hers locked on them. To let her eyes drift to his mouth would have been her downfall. The fingers at her neck tightened, then relaxed and dropped away. Seizing the moment, Cassidy stepped back. The narrowness of her escape shook her, and she dragged her hand through her hair.

Colin watched her, then folded his arms across his chest. "I wonder if you had more difficulty fighting yourself or me."

"So do I," Cassidy replied with impulsive candor.

He tilted his head at her response and studied her. "You're an honest one, Cassidy. Mind how honest you are with me; I'd have few qualms about taking advantage."

"No, I'm sure you wouldn't." After blowing out a long breath, Cassidy straightened her shoulders. "I don't suppose that could have been avoided forever," she began practically. "But now that it hasn't been, and it's done, it shouldn't happen again." Her brow furrowed as Colin tossed back his head and roared with laughter. "Did I say something funny?"

"Cass, you're unique." Before she could respond, he had moved to her and had taken her shoulders in his hands. He kneaded them quickly in a friendly manner. "That streak of British practicality will always war with the passionate Celt."

"You're romanticizing," she claimed and lifted her chin.

"The door's been opened, Cassidy." She frowned because his words reminded her of her earlier thoughts. "Better for you perhaps if we'd kept it locked." He shook her once, rapidly. "Yes, it's done. The door won't stay closed now. It'll happen again." He released her then stepped back, but their eyes remained joined. "Go on now, while I'm remembering you were frightened."

The strong temptation to step toward him alarmed her. In defense against it, she turned swiftly for the door. "Nine o'clock," he said, and she turned with her hand on the knob.

He stood in the room's center, his thumbs hooked in his front pockets. The sun fell through the skylight, silhouetting his dark attraction. It occurred to Cassidy that if she were wise, she would walk out and never come back.

"Not a coward, are you, Cass?" he taunted softly, as if stealing her thoughts from her brain.

Cassidy tossed her head and snapped her spine straight. "Nine o'clock," she stated coolly then slammed the door behind her.

Chapter 4

As the days passed Cassidy found herself more at ease in the role of artist's model. As for Colin himself, she felt it would be a rare thing for anyone to remain relaxed with him. His temperament was mercurial, with a wide range of degrees. Fury came easily to him, but Cassidy learned humor did as well. As she began to uncover different layers of the man, he became more fascinating.

She justified her concentrated study of Colin Sullivan as a writer's privilege. It was a personality like his — varied, unpredictable, bold — that she needed as grist for her profession. There was nothing between them, she told herself regularly, but an artistic exchange. She reminded herself that he hadn't touched her again, except to set the pose, since the first day he had begun work on the canvas. The stormy kiss was a vivid memory, but only that . . . a memory.

Sitting at her typewriter in her apartment, Cassidy told herself she was fortunate — fortunate to have a job that kept the wolf from the door, and fortunate that Colin Sullivan was absorbed in his work. Cassidy was honest enough to admit she was more than mildly attracted to him. It was much better, she mused, that he was capable of pouring himself into his work to the extent that he barely noticed she was flesh and blood. *Unless I move the pose.* She frowned at the reflection of her desk lamp in the window.

Being attracted to him is perfectly natural, she decided. I'm not behaving like my predecessor with the milky skin and falling in love with him. I'm much too sensible. *Don't be so smug,* a voice whispered inside her head. Cassidy's frown became a scowl. I *am* sensible. I won't make a fool of myself over Colin Sullivan. He has his art and his Gail Kingsley. I have my work. Cassidy glanced down at the blank sheet of paper in her typewriter and sighed. But he keeps interfering with it. No more, she vowed then shifted in her seat until she was comfortably settled. I'm going to finish this chapter tonight without another thought of Sullivan.

At once the keys on her typewriter began to clatter with the movement of her thoughts. Once begun, she became totally involved, lost in the characters of her own devising. The love scene developed on her pages as she unconsciously called on her own feelings for her words. The scene moved with the same lightning speed as had the embrace with Colin. Now Cassidy was in control, urging her characters toward each other, propelling their destinies. It was as she wanted, as she planned, and she never noticed the influence of the man she had vowed to think no more about. The scene was nearly finished when a knock sounded on her door. She swore in annoyance.

"Who is it?" she called out and stopped typing in midsentence. She found it simpler to pick up her thoughts when returning to them that way.

"Hey, Cassidy." Jeff Mullans stuck his friendly, red-bearded face through her door. "Got a minute?"

Because he was her neighbor and she was fond of him, Cassidy pushed away the urge to sigh and smiled instead. "Sure."

He eased himself, a guitar and a six-pack of beer through the door. "Can I put some stuff in your fridge? Mine's busted again. It's like the Mojave Desert in there."

"Go ahead." Cassidy spun her chair until she faced him, then quirked her brow. "I see you brought all your valuables. I didn't know your six-string needed refrigeration."

"Just the six-pack," he countered with a grin as he marched back into her tiny kitchen. "And you're the only one in the building I'd trust with it. Wow, Cassidy, don't you believe in real food? All that's in here's a quart of juice, two carrots and half a stick of oleo."

"Is nothing sacred?"

"Come next door and I'll fix you up with a decent meal." Jeff came back into the room holding only his guitar. "I got tacos and stale doughnuts. Jelly-filled."

"It sounds marvelous, but I really have to finish this chapter."

Jeff's fingers pawed at his beard. "Don't know what you're missing. Heard anything from New York?" After glancing at the papers scattered over her desk, he settled Indian-fashion on the floor. He cradled his guitar in his lap.

"There seems to be a conspiracy of silence on the East Coast." Cassidy sighed, shrugged and tucked up her feet. "It's early days yet, I know, but patience isn't my strong suit."

"You'll make it, Cassidy, you've got something." He began to strum idly as he spoke. His music was simple and soothing. "Something that makes the people you write about important. If your novel is as good as that magazine story, you're on your way."

Cassidy smiled, touched by the easy sincerity of the compliment. "You wouldn't like to apply for a job as an editor in a New York publishing house, would you?"

"You don't need me, babe." He grinned and shook back his red hair. "Besides, I'm an up-and-coming songwriter and star performer."

"I've heard that." Cassidy leaned back in her chair. It occurred to her suddenly that Colin might like to paint Jeff Mullans. He'd be the perfect subject for him — the blinding red hair and beard, the soft contrast of gray eyes, the loving way the long hands caressed the guitar as he sat on her wicker rug. Yes, Colin would paint him precisely like this, she decided, in faded, frayed jeans with a polished guitar on his lap.

"Cassidy?"

"Sorry, I took a side trip. Have you got any gigs lined up?"

"Two next week. What about your gig with the artist?" Jeff tightened his bass string fractionally, tested it then continued to play. "I've seen his stuff . . . some of it, anyway. It's incredible." He tilted his head when he smiled at her. "How does it feel to be put on canvas by one of the new masters?"

"It's an odd feeling, Jeff. I've tried to pin it down, but . . ." She trailed off and brought her knees up, resting her heels on the edge of the chair. "I'm never certain it's me he's seeing when he's working. I'm not certain I'll see myself in the finished portrait." She frowned then shrugged it away. "Maybe he's only using part of me, the way I use parts of people I've met in characterizations."

"What's he like?" Jeff asked, watching her eyes drift with her thought. The glow of her desk lamp threw an aura around her head.

"He's fascinating," she murmured, all but forgetting she was speaking aloud. "He looks like a pirate, all dashing and dangerous with the most incredible blue eyes I've ever seen. And his hands are beautiful. There's no other word for them; they're perfectly beautiful."

Her voice softened, and her eyes began to dream. "He exudes a thoughtless sort of sensuality. It seems more obvious when he's working. I suppose it's because he's being driven by his own power then, and is somehow separate from the rest of us. He tells me to talk, and I talk about whatever comes into my head." She moved her shoulders then rested her chin on her knees. "But I don't know if he hears me. He has a dreadful temper, and when he rages his speech slips back to Ireland. It's almost worth the storm to hear it. He's outrageously selfish and unbearably arrogant and utterly charming. Each time I'm with him I find a bit more, uncover another layer, and yet I doubt I'd really know him if I had years to learn."

There was silence for a moment, with only Jeff's music. "You're really hung up on him," he observed.

Cassidy snapped back with a jolt. Her violet eyes widened in surprise as she straightened in the chair. "Why, no, of course not. I'm simply . . . simply . . ." *Simply what, Cassidy?* she demanded of herself. "Simply interested in what makes him the way he is," she answered and hugged her knees. "That's all."

"Okay, babe, you know best." Jeff stood in an easy fluid motion, the guitar merely an extension of his arm. "Just watch out." He smiled, leaned over and cupped her chin. "He might be a great artist, but if the gossip columns are to be believed, he's very much a man, too. You're a fine-looking lady, and you might as well be fresh from the farm."

"I'd hardly call four years at Berkeley fresh from the farm," Cassidy countered.

"Only someone utterly naive could evade every pass I make and still make me like her." Jeff closed the distance and gave her a gentle invitation of a kiss. It was as pleasant and as soothing as his music. Cassidy's heartbeat stayed steady. "No dice, huh?" he asked when he lifted his head. "Think of the rent we could save if we moved in together."

Cassidy tugged on his beard. "You're only lusting after my refrigerator."

"A lot you know," he scoffed and headed for the door. "I'm going home to write something painfully sad and poignant."

"Good grief, I'm always inspiring someone these days."

"Don't get cocky," Jeff advised then closed the door behind him.

Cassidy's smile faded as she stared off into space. Hung up on, she repeated mentally. What a silly phrase. In any case, I'm not hung up on Colin. Can't a woman express an interest in a man without someone reading more into it? Thoughtfully she ran her fingertip over her bottom lip and brought back the feel of Jeff's kiss.

Easy, undisturbing, painless. What sort of chemistry made one man's kiss pleasant and another's exhilarating? The smart woman would go for the pleasant, Cassidy decided, knowing Jeff would be basically kind and gentle. Only an idiot would want a man who was bound to bring hurt and heartache.

With a quick shake of her head she swung back to her typewriter and began to work. Her fingers had barely begun to transfer her thoughts when a knock sounded again. Cassidy rolled her eyes to the ceiling.

"You can't possibly be finished writing a painfully sad and poignant song," she called out and continued to type. "And the beer certainly isn't cold yet."

"I can't argue with either of those statements."

Cassidy spun her chair quickly and stared at Colin. He stood in her opened doorway, negligently leaning against the jamb and watching her. There was light amusement on his face and male appreciation in his eyes as they roamed over her skin. It was scantily covered in brief shorts and a T-shirt that had shrunk in the basement laundry. His lazy survey brought out a blush before she found her tongue.

"What are you doing here?"

"Enjoying the view," he answered and stepped inside. He closed the door at his back then lifted a brow. "Don't you know better than to keep your door unlatched?"

"I'm always losing my key and locking myself out, so I . . ." Cassidy stopped because she realized how ridiculous she sounded. One day, she promised herself, I'll learn to think before I speak. "There isn't anything in here worth stealing," she said.

Colin shook his head. "How wrong you are. Wear your key around your neck, Cass, but keep your door locked." Her brain formed an indignant retort, but before she could vocalize it he spoke again. "Who did you think I was when I knocked?"

"A songwriter with a faulty refrigerator. How did you know where I lived?"

"Your address is on your manuscript." He gestured with the thick envelope before setting it down.

Cassidy glanced at the familiar bundle with some surprise. She had assumed Colin had forgotten her manuscript as soon as she'd given it to him. Suddenly it occurred to her why she hadn't asked him before if he had read it, or what he'd thought of it. His criticism would be infinitely harder to bear than an impersonal rejection slip from a faceless editor. Abruptly nervous, she looked up at him. Any critique she was expecting wasn't forthcoming.

Colin wandered the room, toying with an arrangement of dried flowers, examining a snapshot in a silver frame, peering out of the window at her view of the city.

"Can I get you something?" she asked automatically then remembered Jeff's inventory of her refrigerator. She bit her lip. "Coffee," she added quickly, knowing she could provide it as long as he took it black.

Colin turned from the window and began to wander again. "You have a proper eye for color, Cass," he told her. "And an enviable way of making a home from an apartment. I've always found them soulless devices, lacking in privacy and character." He lifted a small mirror framed with sea shells. "Fisherman's Wharf," he concluded and glanced at her. "It must be a particular haunt of yours."

"Yes, I suppose. I love the city in general and that part of it in particular." She smiled as she thought of it. "There's so much life there. The boats are all crammed in beside each other, and I like to imagine

88

where they've been or where they're going." As soon as the words were spoken Cassidy felt foolish. They sounded romantic when she had been taking great pains to prove to Colin she was not. He smiled at her, and her embarrassment became something more dangerous. "I'll make coffee," she said quickly and started to rise.

"No, don't bother." Colin laid a hand on her shoulder to keep her seated then glanced at her desk. It was cluttered with papers and notes and reference books. "I'm interrupting your work. Intolerable."

"It seems to be the popular thing to do tonight." Cassidy shook off her discomfort and smiled as he continued to pace the room. "It's all right because I was nearly done, otherwise I suppose I'd behave as rudely as you do when you're interrupted." She enjoyed the look he gave her, the ironical lift of his brow, the light tilt of a smile on his mouth.

"And how rudely is that?"

"Abominably. Please sit, Colin. These floors are thin, you'll wear them through." She gestured to a chair, but he perched on the edge of her desk.

"I finished your book tonight."

"Yes, I thought perhaps that's why you

brought the manuscript back." She spoke calmly enough, but when he made no response she moaned in frustration. "Please, Colin, I'm no good with torture. I'd confess everything I knew before they stuck the first bamboo shoot under my fingernail. I'm a marshmallow. No, wait!" She held up both hands as he started to speak. She rose and then took a quick turn around the room. "If you hated it, I'll only be devastated for a short time. I'm certain I'll learn to function again . . . well, nearly certain. I want you to be frank. I don't want any platitudes or cushioned letdowns." She pushed her mane of hair back with both hands, letting her fingers linger on her temples a moment. "And for heaven's sake, don't tell me it was interesting. That's the worst. The absolute worst!"

"Are you finished?" he asked mildly.

Cassidy blew out a long breath, tugged her hand through her hair and nodded. "Yes, I think so."

"Come here, Cass." She obeyed instantly because his voice was quiet and gentle. Their eyes were level, and he took her hands in his. "I haven't mentioned the book until now because I wanted to read it when I wouldn't be interrupted. I thought it best not to talk about it until I finished." His thumbs ran absently over the back of her hands. "You have something rare, Cass, something elusive. Talent. It's not something they taught you at Berkeley, it's something you were born with. Your college years polished it, perhaps, disciplined it, but you provided the raw material."

Cassidy released her breath. Astonishing, she thought, that the opinion of a man known barely a week should have such weight. Jeff's opinion had pleased her; Colin's had left her speechless.

"I don't know what to say." She shook her head helplessly. "That sounds trite, I know, but it's true." Her eyes drifted past him to the disorder of papers on her desk. "Sometimes you just want to chuck it all. It just isn't worth the pain, the struggle."

"And you would choose to be a writer," Colin said.

"No, I never had any choice." She brought her eyes back to his. The violet glowed almost black in the shadowed light. "If anything, it picked me. Did you choose to be an artist, Colin?"

He studied her a moment, then shook his head. "No." He turned her hands, palms up, and looked at them with lowered brows. "There are things that come to us whether we ask for them or not. Do you believe in destiny, Cass?"

She moistened her lips, finding them suddenly dry, then swallowed. "Yes." The single syllable was little more than a breath.

"Of course, I was certain you did." He lifted his eyes and locked them on hers. Cassidy's heartbeat jumped skittishly. "Do you think it's our destiny to be lovers, Cassidy?" Her mouth opened but no words came out. She shook her head in mute denial. "You're a poor liar," he observed; then, cupping her chin in his palm, he moved his lips to hers. In direct contrast to the ease and pleasantness of Jeff's kiss, this brought a pain that seemed to vibrate in every cell of her body. Defensively Cassidy jerked her head back.

"Don't!"

"Why?" he countered, and his voice was soft. "A kiss is a simple thing, a meeting of lips."

"No, it's not simple," Cassidy protested, feeling herself being pulled to him by his eyes only. "You take more."

He kissed one cheek, then the other, barely touching her skin. Cassidy's eyelids fluttered down. "Only as much as you'll give me, Cass. That much and no more."

His lips moved over hers, teasing, persuading, until her blood thundered in her brain. His fingers were gentle on her face. "You taste of things I'd forgotten," he murmured. "Fresh, young things. Kiss me, Cass, I've a need for you."

With a moan, half-despair, half-wonder, she answered his need.

The flames that leapt between them were intense and wild. Her brain sent out quick, desperate protests and was ignored. A hunger for him drove her; her mouth became urgent and searching as his hands began to explore her soft curves. The fear she felt only added to her excitement, the exquisite terror of losing control. She was overwhelmed by a primitive need, an ageless necessity. When their lips parted and met again, hers ached for the joining.

Abruptly he tore his mouth from hers and buried it against her neck. Cassidy shuddered from the onslaught even as she tilted back her head to offer him more. With his teeth he brought her skin alive with delicious pain. His hands found their way under her shirt, running up her rib cage. With his thumbs he stroked the sides of her breast while she strained against him.

Her joints went fluid, leaving her helpless but for his support. For a moment, when their lips met again, there was nothing she had that was not his. The offer was complete and unconditional. Slowly, with his hands on her shoulders, Colin drew her away. Her lashes fluttered up then down, before she found the strength to open her eyes. His expression was dark and forbidding. Briefly his hands tightened.

"It seems you were right," he began in a voice thick with desire. "A kiss isn't a simple thing. I want you, Cass, and you'd best know nothing in heaven or hell will keep me from taking you when I've a mind to." His hands relaxed, the grip becoming a caress. "When the painting's finished, we'll have no choice but to meet our destinies."

"No." Frightened, disturbed by feelings that were too intense, Cassidy pulled out of his arms. She dragged a trembling hand through her hair, and her breath came quickly. "No, Colin, I won't be the latest in your string of lovers. I won't! I think more of myself than that. That's something you'd best understand." She stepped away from him, her shoulders straightening with inherent pride.

Colin's eyes narrowed. She could see his temper rising. "It should be an interesting contest." He took a step forward and grabbed a handful of her hair. With a quick jerk he brought her face to his, then gave her a hard, brief kiss. Cassidy's breath trembled out, but she kept her eyes steady. "Time will tell, Cass my love. Now it's late, nearly midnight, and I'd best be on my way." Lifting her hand, he brushed her fingers with his lips. "Sinning is much more appealing after midnight." With another careless smile, he turned for the door. Reaching it, he pushed the latch so that it would engage when he shut it. "Find your keys," he ordered and was gone.

Chapter 5

Another week passed without any clash between Colin and Cassidy. She had returned to his studio the day after his visit to her apartment determined to resist him. She'd spoken the truth when she'd told him she wouldn't be one of his lovers.

All her life she had waited for a relationship with depth and permanence. Her own ideals and her dedication to her studies had kept her aloof from men, and her aloofness had prolonged her naiveté. She'd grown up with only a father and had never closely witnessed the commitment of a man and a woman to each other. She had watched her father enjoy several light relationships as she'd grown up, but none of the women in his life had become important to him. Watching him drift through life with only his work, Cassidy had vowed she would find someone one day to share hers.

She didn't consider her vow romantic, but as necessary to her soul as food was to her body. Until she found what she searched for, she would wait. Before Colin there had never been any temptation to do otherwise. Still, when she returned to his studio, she was prepared to stand firm against him. Her preparation proved unnecessary.

Colin spoke to her only briefly, and when he set the pose his touch was impersonal. But there seemed to be some surge of emotion just under the surface of his face, something that just stirred the air. Whether it was temper or passion or excitement, Cassidy had no way of knowing. She knew only she was vitally aware of it . . . and of him.

They passed the days with only what needed to be said, and long gaps of silence filled the sessions. By the end of the week Cassidy's nerves were stretched taut. She wondered if Colin felt the tension, or if it was simply within her. He seemed intent only on the painting.

The sun fell over Cassidy warmly, but her muscles were growing stiff from holding the pose. Colin stood behind his easel, and she watched his brush move from palette to canvas. He could work for hours without a moment's rest. Cassidy tried to imagine how he had painted her.

Will I hang in The Gallery or face the wall in a corner up here until he decides what to do with me? she thought. Will I be sold for some astronomical price and hang in a manor house in England? What will he title me? *Woman in White. Woman with Violets.* She tried to imagine being discussed and pondered over by an art class in a university. A century from now, will someone see me in some dusty gallery and wonder who I was or what I was thinking when he painted me?

The idea gave Cassidy an odd feeling, one she was not certain wholly pleased her. How much of her soul could Colin see, and how much would be revealed with oil and canvas? Would she, in essence, be as naked as the model who'd lounged on the couch?

Colin swore roundly, snapping her attention back to him. Her eyes widened as he slammed down his palette.

"You've moved the pose." He stalked toward her as her mouth opened to form an apology. "Hold still, blast you," he ordered curtly, adjusting her shoulders with impatient hands. His brows were lowered in annoyance. "I won't tolerate fidgeting."

Cassidy's mouth snapped shut on her apology. Swift and heated, her temper rose.

With one quick jerk she pulled out of his hands. "Don't you speak to me that way, Sullivan." She threw her nosegay on the windowsill and glared at him. "I was not fidgeting, and if I were, it would be because I'm human, not a — a robot or a dime-store dummy." She tossed her head, effectively destroying his arrangement of her hair. "I'm sure it's difficult to understand a mere mortal when one is so lofty and godlike, but we can't all be perfect."

"Your opinions are neither requested nor desired." Colin's voice was as cold as his eyes were heated. "The only thing I require from a model is that she hold still." He took her shoulders again, firmly. "Keep your temper to yourself when I'm working."

"Go paint a tree, then," she invited furiously. "It won't give you any back talk." Cassidy turned to stalk to the dressing room, but Colin grabbed her arm and spun her around. His face was alive with temper.

"No one walks away from me."

"Is that so?" Cassidy lifted her chin, infuriated with his arrogance. "Watch this." She turned her back on him only to be whirled around again before she had taken two steps. "Let go of me," she ordered as blood surged angrily under her skin.

Nerves that had been stretched for a week strained to the breaking point. "I've nothing more to say, and I'm through holding your blasted pose for the day."

His grip on her arm tightened. "Very well, but there's more between us than painting and talking, isn't there?" He bit off the words as he dragged her against him.

Cassidy's heart jumped to her throat when she felt the violence of his fingers against her skin. She saw that temper ruled him now, a temper sharp enough to cut through any protest she could make. He was a man of passion, and she was aware that his darker side could carry them both past the turning point. In a desperate attempt to hold him off, Cassidy arched away from him. Even as she made the move, his mouth crushed hers. She tasted his fury.

Her sounds of protest were muffled, her arms pinioned by his. In her throat, her heart thudded with the knowledge that she was totally at his mercy. His lips were bruising, unyielding, as his tongue penetrated her mouth. The kiss became as intimate as it was savage. When she tried to turn her face from his, he gripped her hair tightly and held her still. His mouth was hard and hot and ruthless. Behind her closed lids, a dull red mist swirled. For the first time in her life, Cassidy feared she would faint. Her protests became slighter. Colin took more.

He was pulling her too deep too quickly, down dark corridors, beyond the border of thought and into sensation. There was no gentleness on the journey, only hard, uncompromising demand. Unable to fight him any longer, Cassidy went limp. She made no struggle when his hand moved to unfasten the dress. Her body was consumed by fire, instinctively responding to his touch. The knock on the studio door vibrated like a cannon through the room. Ignoring it, Colin continued to ravish her mouth.

"Colin." Dimly Cassidy heard Gail Kingsley's voice and the sound of another knock. "There's someone here to see you."

With a savage oath, Colin tore his mouth from Cassidy's. He released her abruptly, and freed of support she staggered and fell against him. Cursing again, he took her arms and held her away, but his words halted as he studied her wide, frightened eyes.

Her mouth was trembling, swollen by his demands. Her breath sobbed in and out of her lungs as she clung to him for balance.

"Colin, don't be nasty." Gail's voice sounded with practiced patience through the door. "You must be pretty well finished by now."

"All right, blast it!" he called out brusquely to Gail but kept his eyes on Cassidy. Leading her by the arm, he walked to the dressing room. Inside he turned her again to face him. In silence she looked up, struggling to balance her system and discipline her breathing. The need to weep was tearing at her.

An expression came and went in Colin's eyes. "Change," he said in a quiet voice. He seemed to hesitate, as if to say more, then he turned away. When he shut the door, Cassidy turned to face the wall.

She let the trembling run its course. Several minutes passed before the voices in the studio penetrated.

There was Gail's quick, nervous tone and Colin's, calm now, without any trace of the temper of passion that had dominated it before. An unfamiliar voice mixed with theirs. It was light and male with an Italian accent. Cassidy concentrated on the voices rather than the words. Turning, she stared at her own reflection. What she saw left her stunned.

Color had not yet returned to her cheeks, leaving them nearly as white as the dress she wore. Her eyes were haunted. It was the look of utter vulnerability that disturbed her the most; the look of a woman accepting defeat.

No. No, I won't. She pressed her palm over the face in the glass. *He'll win nothing that way, and we both know it.* Quickly she stripped out of the dress and began to pull on her clothes. The straight, uncompromising lines of her khakis and button-down shirt made her appear less frail, and she began a careful repair of her face. The conversation in the outer room started to penetrate her thoughts. The first moments of eavesdropping were unconscious.

"An interesting use of color, Colin. You seem to be working toward a rather dream-like effect." Hearing Gail's comment, Cassidy realized they were discussing the painting. She frowned as she applied blusher to her cheeks. *He lets her look at it,* she thought resentfully. *Why not me?* "It seems almost sentimental. That should be a surprise to the art world."

"Sentimental, yes." The Italian voice cut in while Cassidy now eavesdropped shamelessly. "But there is passion in this play of color here, and a rather cool practicality in the line of the dress. I'm intrigued, Colin; I can't figure out your intention."

"I have more than one," Cassidy heard him answer in his dry, ironic tone.

"How well I know." The Italian chuckled then made a sound of curiosity. "You have not begun the face."

"No." Cassidy recognized the dismissal in the word, but the Italian ignored it.

"She interests me . . . and you, too, it appears. She would be beautiful, of course, and young enough to suit the dress and the violets. Still, she must have something more." Cassidy waited for Colin's reply, but none came. The Italian continued, undaunted. "Will you keep her hidden, my friend?"

"Yes, Colin, where is Cassidy?" Gail's question held an undertone of amusement that made Cassidy's eyes narrow. "You know she'd adore meeting Vince." She gave a light laugh. "She is rather a sweet-looking thing. Don't tell me we ran her off?"

Thoroughly annoyed with the condescending description, Cassidy turned and opened the door. "Not at all," she said and gave the trio by the easel a brilliant smile. "And of course I'd adore meeting Vince."

She saw Gail's eyes glitter with a quick fury then shifted her gaze to Colin. His face told her nothing, and again her gaze shifted.

The man beside Colin was nearly a head shorter, but his lean build and proud carriage gave the illusion of height. His hair was as dark as Colin's, but straight, and his eyes were darkly brown against the olive of his skin. He had smooth, handsome features, and when he smiled he was all but irresistible.

"Ah, *bella.*" The compliment was a sigh before he crossed the room to take both of Cassidy's hands in his. "*Bellisima.* But of course, she is perfection. Where did you find her, Colin?" he demanded as his eyes caressed her face. "I will go and set up camp there until I find a prize of my own."

Cassidy laughed, amused by his undisguised flirtation. "In the fog," she told him when Colin remained silent. "I thought he was a mugger."

"Ah, my angel, he is much worse than that." Vince turned to Colin with a grin but retained Cassidy's hand. "He is a black Irish dog whose paintings I buy because I have nothing better to do with my money."

Colin lifted a brow as he moved to join them. "Vince, Cassidy St. John. Cass,

Vincente Clemenza, the duke of Maracanti."

At the introduction Cassidy's eyes grew wide. "Ah, now you have impressed her with my title." Vince's teeth flashed into a grin. "How accommodating of you." With perfect charm he lifted both of Cassidy's hands to his lips. "My pleasure, *signorina*. Will you marry me?"

"I've always thought I'd make a spectacular duchess. Do I curtsy?" she asked, smiling at him over their joined hands. "I'm not certain I know how."

"Vince normally requires that one kneel and kiss his ring." At the comment, Cassidy let her eyes drift to Colin. His gaze was dark and brooding on her face. Fractionally, she lifted her chin. Though he said nothing, she sensed his acknowledgment of the gesture.

"You exaggerate, my friend." Vince released Cassidy's hands then laid his own on Colin's shoulder. "As never before, I envy you your gift. You will give me first claim on the portrait."

Colin's eyes remained fixed on Cassidy's face. "There's been a prior claim."

"Indeed." Vince shrugged. The movement was at once elegant and foreign. "I shall have to outbid my competition."

There was an inflection in his tone of a man used to having his own way. Hearing it Cassidy wondered how he and Colin dealt together with such apparent amiability.

"Vince wanted to see *Janeen*," Gail cut in and moved across the room to a stack of canvases.

"If you'll excuse me, then," Cassidy began, but Vince scooped up her hand again.

"No, *madonna*, stay. Come peruse the master's work with me." Without waiting for her assent he urged her across the room.

Gail took a canvas then propped it on an easel. It was the portrait of the nude with the milky skin. Cassidy glanced up to see Gail smiling.

"Cassidy's predecessor," she announced then stepped back to stand with Colin. Cassidy recognized the proprietary nature of the gesture. She turned her attention back to the portrait without looking at Colin.

"An exquisite animal," Vince murmured. "One would say a woman without boundaries. There is quite an attractive wickedness about her." He turned his head to smile at Cassidy. "What do you think?"

"It's magnificent," she replied immediately. "She makes me uncomfortable, and yet I envy her confidence in her own sexuality. I think she would intimidate most men . . . and enjoy it."

"Your model appears to be an astute judge of character." Vince rubbed his thumb absently over Cassidy's knuckles. "Yes, I want it. And the Faylor Gail showed me downstairs. He shows promise. Now, madonna . . ." He turned to face Cassidy again. His eyes were dark and appreciative. "You will have dinner with me tonight? The city is a lonely place without a beautiful woman."

Cassidy smiled, but before she could speak Colin laid a hand on her shoulder. "The paintings are yours, Vince. My model isn't."

"Ah." Vince's one syllable was ripe with meaning. Cassidy's eyes narrowed with fury. Smoothly Colin turned to take the painting from the easel.

"Have someone package this and the Faylor for Vince," he told Gail as he handed her the canvas. "I'll be down shortly and we'll discuss terms."

Without a word Gail crossed the studio and swung through the door. Vince watched her with a thoughtful eye then turned back to Cassidy.

"*Arrivederci,* Cassidy St. John." He kissed her hand then sighed with regret. "It seems I must find my own dream in the fog. I will expect a bargain price to soothe my crushing disappointment, my friend." He shot a look at Colin as he moved to the door. "If you are ever in Italy, madonna . . ." With a final smile he left them.

Trembling with rage, Cassidy turned on Colin the moment the door closed. "How *dare* you?" Now she had no need of blusher to bring color to her cheeks. "How dare you imply such a thing?"

"I merely told Vince he could have the paintings but not my current model," Colin countered. Carelessly he moved across the room and covered Cassidy's portrait. "Any implication was purely coincidental."

"Oh, no!" Cassidy followed him, propelled by fury. "That was no coincidence. You knew precisely what you were doing. I won't tolerate that sort of interference from you, Sullivan." She took a finger and poked him in the chest. "I'm perfectly free to see whomever I choose, whenever I choose, and I won't have you implying otherwise."

Colin hooked his hands in his pockets. For a moment he studied her face in silence. When he spoke it was with perfect calm. "You're very young and remarkably naive. Vince is an old friend and a good one. He's also a charming rake, if you'll forgive the archaic term. He has no scruples with women."

"And you do?" Cassidy retorted in an instant of blind heat. She saw Colin stiffen, saw his eyes flare and the muscles in his face tense. For the first time she witnessed his calculated control of his temper.

"Your point, Cass," he said softly. "Well taken." His hands stayed in his pockets as he watched her. "Don't come back until Thursday," he told her and turned to walk to the door. "I need a day or two."

Cassidy stood alone in the empty studio. I may have scored a point, she thought wretchedly, but this victory isn't sweet. She was drained, physically as well as emotionally. She returned to the dressing room for her purse. Colin wasn't the only one who needed a day or two.

"Oh, what luck, I've caught you." Gail swept into the studio just as Cassidy emerged from the dressing room. "I thought we might have a little chat." Gail shot her a quick, flashing smile and leaned back against the closed door. "Just us two," she added.

Cassidy sighed with undisguised weariness. "Not now," she said and shifted her purse to her shoulder. "I've had enough temperament for one day."

"I'll make it brief, then, and you can be on your way." Gail spoke pleasantly enough, but Cassidy felt the antagonism just below the surface.

It's best not to argue, Cassidy decided. It's best to hear her out, agree with everything she says and go quietly. That's the sensible thing to do.

She gave her what she hoped was an inoffensive smile. "All right, go ahead, then."

Gail took a quick, sweeping survey. "I'm afraid perhaps I haven't made myself clear . . . about myself and Colin." Her voice was patient — teacher to student. Cassidy ignored a surge of annoyance and nodded.

"Colin and I have been together for quite some time. We meet a certain need in each other. Over the years he's had his share of flirtations, which I'm quite capable of overlooking. In many cases these relationships were intensified for the press." She shrugged a gauze-covered shoulder. "Colin's romantic image helps maintain the mystique of the artist. I'll sanction anything when it helps his career. I understand him."

As if unable to remain still for more than

short spurts, Gail began to roam the room.

"I'm afraid I don't see why you're telling me this," Cassidy began. The last thing she needed to hear at the moment was how experienced Colin Sullivan was with women.

"Let's you and I understand each other, too." Gail stopped pacing and faced Cassidy again. Her eyes were hard and cold. "As long as Colin's doing this painting, I have to tolerate you. I know better than to interfere with his work. But if you get in my way . . ." She wrapped her fingers around the strap of Cassidy's purse. "I can find ways of removing people who get in my way."

"I'm sure you can," Cassidy returned evenly. "I'm afraid you'll find I don't remove easily." She pried Gail's fingers from her strap. "Your relationship with Colin is your own affair. I've no intention of interfering with it. Not," she added as a satisfied smile tilted the corner of Gail's mouth, "because you threaten me. You don't intimidate me, Gail. Actually, I feel rather sorry for you."

Cassidy ignored Gail's harsh intake of breath and continued. "Your lack of confidence where Colin is concerned is pathetic. I'm no threat to you. A blind man could see he's only interested in what he puts on that canvas over there." She flung out a hand and pointed to the covered portrait. "I interest him as a *thing,* not as a person." She felt a quick slash of pain as her own statement came home to her. She continued to speak, though the words rushed out in desperation. "I won't interfere with you because I'm not in love with Colin, and I have no intention of ever being in love with him."

Whirling, she darted through the back door of the studio, slamming it at her back. Only after she had gulped in enough air to steady her nerves did Cassidy realize she had lied.

Chapter 6

For the next two days Cassidy buried herself in her work. She was determined to give herself a time of peace, a time of rest for her emotions. She knew she needed to cut herself off from Colin to accomplish it. The disruption of their day-to-day contact wasn't enough. She knew she needed to block him from her mind. In addition, Cassidy forced herself not to consider the knowledge that had come to her after the scene with Gail. She wouldn't think of being in love with Colin or of the circumstances that made her love impossible. For two days she would pretend she'd never met him.

Cassidy wrote frantically. All her fears and pain and passion were expressed in her words. She worked late into the night, until she could be certain there would be no dreams to haunt her. When she slept, she slept deeply, exhausted by her own drive. More than once she forgot to eat.

On the second day it began to rain. There was a solid gray wall outside Cassidy's window of which she remained totally unaware. Below, pedestrians scrambled about under umbrellas.

Cassidy's concentration was so complete that when a hand touched her shoulder, she screamed.

"Wow, Cassidy, I'm sorry." Jeff tried to look apologetic but grinned instead. "I knocked and called you twice. You were totally absorbed."

Cassidy held a hand against her heart as if to keep it in place. She took two deep breaths. "It's all right. We all need to be terrified now and again. It keeps the blood moving. Is it your refrigerator?"

Jeff grimaced as he ran a finger down her nose. "Is that where you think my heart is? In your refrigerator? Cassidy, I'm a sensitive guy, my mother'll tell you." Cassidy smiled, leaning back in her chair.

"I've got that gig in the coffeehouse down the street tonight. Come with me."

"Oh, Jeff, I'd love to, but —" She began to make her excuses with a gesture at the papers on her desk. Jeff cut her off.

"Listen, you've been chained to this machine for two days. When are you coming up for air?"

She shrugged and poked a finger at her dictionary. "I've got to go back to the studio tomorrow, and —"

"All the more reason for a break tonight. You're pushing yourself, babe. Take a rest." Jeff watched her face carefully and pressed his advantage. "I could use a friendly face in the audience, you know. We rising stars are very insecure." He grinned through his beard.

Cassidy sighed then smiled. "All right, but I can't stay late."

"I play from eight to eleven," he told her then ruffled her hair. "You can be home and tucked into bed before midnight."

"Okay, I'll be there at eight." Cassidy glanced down at her watch, frowned then tapped its face with her fingertips. "What time is it? My watch stopped at two-fifteen."

"A.M. or P.M.?" Jeff asked dryly. He shook his head. "It's after seven. Hey." He gave her a shrewd look. "Have you eaten?"

Cassidy cast her mind back and recalled an apple at noon. "No, not really."

With a snort of disgust Jeff hauled her to her feet. "Come on with me now, and I'll spring for a quick hamburger."

Cassidy pushed her hair back out of her face. "Golly, I haven't had such a generous offer for a long time."

"Just get a coat," Jeff retorted, stalking to her door. "In case you haven't noticed, it's pouring outside."

Cassidy glanced out her window. "So it is," she agreed. She pulled a yellow slicker out of the closet and dragged it on. "Can I have a cheeseburger?" she asked Jeff as she breezed past him.

"Women. Never satisfied." He closed the door behind them.

The rain didn't bother Cassidy. It was refreshing after her hibernation. The hurried cheeseburger and soft drink were a banquet after the scant meals of the past two days. The smoky, crowded coffeehouse gave her a taste of humanity that she relished after her solitude.

Seated near the back, she drank thick café au lait and listened to Jeff's soothing, introspective music. The evening had grown late when she realized she had relaxed her guard. Colin had slipped over her barrier without her being aware. He stood clearly in her mind's eye. Once he had breached her defenses, Cassidy knew it was useless to attempt to force him out again. She closed her eyes a moment, then opened them, accepting the inevitable. She could not avoid thinking of him forever.

Colin Sullivan was a brilliant artist. He was a confident man who twisted life to suit himself. He had wit and charm and sensitivity. He was selfish and arrogant and

117

totally dedicated to his work. He was thoughtless and domineering and capable of violence.

And I love him completely.

Cassidy trembled with a sigh, then stared into her coffee. I'm an idiot, a romantic fool who knew the pitfalls then fell into one anyway. I see he has a lover, I understand he sees me as important only as a subject for his painting. I'm aware he would make love to me without his heart ever being touched. I know there've been dozens of women in his life, and none of them have lasted.

No, not even Gail, she mused, for all her claims. She's just another woman who's touched the corners of his life. Colin's never made a commitment to a woman. Knowing all this, and wanting a healthy, one-to-one relationship with a man, I fall in love with him. Brilliant.

It's insane. He'll trample me. So what do I do? Slowly Cassidy lifted her coffee and sipped. She drifted away from her surroundings.

I have to finish the portrait; I gave my word. It would be impossible to be in the studio together day after day and not speak. I'm not capable of feuding in any case. Her elbows were propped on the table, the cup held between her hands, but her eyes were staring over the rim and into the distance.

Fighting with him is too dangerous because it brings the emotions to the surface. I don't know how deeply inside me he's capable of seeing. I won't humiliate myself or embarrass him with the fact that I've been stupid enough to fall in love with him. The only thing to do is to behave naturally. Hold the pose for him, talk when he asks me to talk and be friendly. The painting seems to be moving well; it should be finished in a few more weeks. Surely I can behave properly for that amount of time. And when it's finished . . .

Her thoughts trailed off into darkness. And when the painting's finished, what? I pick up the pieces, she answered. For a moment her eyes were lost and sad. When the painting's finished and Colin drops out of my life, the universe will still function. What a small thing one person's happiness is, she reflected. What a tiny, finite slice of the whole.

With a sigh Cassidy shook off her thoughts and finished the coffee. Setting down the cup she let herself be stroked by Jeff's quiet music.

★ ★ ★

Cassidy pulled her jacket closer as she stood outside the studio door and searched her bag for the key Colin had given her.

Blasted key, she grumbled silently as she groped for it. She blew her hair from her eyes then pulled out a notepad, three pencils and a linty sourball.

"How did that get in there?" she mumbled. Her eyes flew up when Colin opened the door. "Oh. Hello."

He inclined his head at the greeting then dropped his eyes to her laden hands. "Looking for something?"

Cassidy followed his gaze. Embarrassed, she dumped everything back into her bag and fumbled for poise. "No, I . . . nothing. I didn't think you'd be here so early." She shifted her purse back to her shoulder.

"It appears it's fortunate I am. Have you lost your key, Cass?" There was a smile on his face that made her feel foolish and scatter-brained.

"No, I haven't lost it," she muttered. "I just can't find it." She walked past him into the studio. Her shoulder barely brushed his chest and she felt a jolt of heat. It wasn't going to be as easy as she'd thought. "I'll change," she said briefly then went directly to the dressing room.

When she emerged, Colin was setting his palette and gave her not so much as a glance. His ignoring of her brought a wave of relief. There, you see, she told herself, there's nothing to worry about.

"I'm going to do some work on the face today," Colin stated, still mixing paints. His use of the impersonal pronoun was further proof his thoughts were not on Cassidy St. John. She denied the existence of the ache in her chest. Keeping silent, she waited until he was finished then stood obligingly while he set the pose. She would, she determined, give him absolutely no trouble. But when he cupped her chin in his hand, she stiffened and jerked away.

Colin's eyes heated. "I need to see the shape of your face through my hands." He set the pose again with meticulous care, barely making contact. "It's not enough to see it with my eyes. Do you understand?"

She nodded, feeling foolish. Colin waited a moment then took her chin again, but lightly, with just his fingertips. Cassidy forced herself to remain still. "Relax, Cassidy, I need you relaxed." The patient tone of the order surprised her into obeying. He murmured his approval as his fingers trailed over her skin.

To Cassidy it was an agony of delight. His touch was gentle, though he frowned in concentration. She wondered if he could feel the heat rising to her skin. Colin traced her jawline and ran his fingers over her cheekbones. Cassidy focused on bringing air in and out of her lungs at an even pace. She tried to tell herself that his touch was as impersonal as a doctor's, but when his hand lingered on her cheek she brought her eyes warily to his.

"Hold steady," he commanded briskly, then turned to go to his easel. "Look at me," he ordered as he picked up his palette and brush.

Cassidy obeyed, trying to put her mind on anything but the man who painted her. Even as her eyes met his, she realized it was hopeless. She could not look at him and not see him. She could not be with him and not be aware of him. She could not block him out of her mind with any more success than she could block him out of her heart.

Would it be wrong, she wondered, to let myself dream a little? Would it be wrong to look for some pieces of happiness in the time I have left with him? Unhappiness will come soon enough. Can't I just enjoy being near him and pay the price after he's gone? It seemed a small thing.

Cassidy watched him work, memorizing every part of him. There would come a time, she knew, when she would want the memories. She studied the dark fullness of the hair falling on his forehead and curling over his collar. She studied the black arched brows which were capable of expressing so many moods. The planes of his face fascinated her. His eyes lifted again and again to her face as he painted. There was a fierce concentration in them, an urgency that intensified an already impossible blue.

She couldn't see his hands, but she envisioned them, long and narrow and beautiful. She could feel them learning her face, seeing what perhaps she herself would never see, understanding what she might never understand. If one has to fall foolishly in love, she decided, there couldn't be a more perfect man.

They worked for hours, taking short breaks for Cassidy to stretch her muscles. Colin was always impatient to begin again. She sensed his mood, his excitement, and knew something exceptional was being created. The studio was alive with it. Eagerness, anticipation, tingled in the air.

"The eyes," he muttered and set down

his palette. Quickly he stalked over to her. "Come, I need to see you closer." He pulled her to just behind the easel. "The eyes can be the soul of a portrait."

Colin took her by the shoulders, and his face was barely an inch from hers. The smell of paint and turpentine was sharp in her nostrils. Cassidy knew she would never smell them again without thinking of him.

"Look at me, Cass. Straight on."

She obeyed, though the look of his eyes nearly undid her. It was deep, intruding, reaching past what was offered and seeking the whole. Reflected in his eyes, she saw herself.

I'm a prisoner there, she thought. His. Their breath mingled, and her lips parted, inviting his to close the minute distance. Something flickered and nearly caught flame. Abruptly he stepped back to his canvas.

Cassidy spoke without thinking. "What did you see?"

"Secrets," Colin murmured as he painted. "Dreams. No, don't look away, Cass, it's your dreams I need."

Helplessly Cassidy brought her eyes back. It was far too late for resistance. Setting down his palette and brush, Colin frowned at the canvas for several long moments, then he stepped toward Cassidy and smiled.

"It's perfect. You gave me what I needed."

Cassidy felt a tiny thrill of alarm. "Is it finished?"

"No, but nearly." He lifted her hands and kissed them one at a time. "Soon."

"Soon," she repeated and thought it an ugly word. Quickly she shoved back depression. "Then it must be going well."

"Yes, it's going well."

"But you're not going to let me see it yet."

"I'm superstitious." He gave her hands a gentle squeeze. "Humor me."

"You let Gail see it." Unable to prevent herself, Cassidy let resentment slip into her tone.

"Gail's an artist," Colin pointed out. He released her hands then patted her cheek. "Not the model."

With a sigh of defeat Cassidy turned to wander the room. "You must have painted her . . . at one time or other," she commented. "She's so striking, so vital."

"She can't hold a pose for five minutes," Colin said. He began to clean his brushes at the worktable.

Smiling, Cassidy leaned on the windowsill. "Do you have a hard time with your seascapes?" she asked him. "Or do you simply command the water and clouds to stop fidgeting? I believe you could do it." She stretched then lifted the weight of her hair from her neck. With an expansive sigh, she let it fall again to tumble as it chose. The sun shimmered through its shades.

When she turned her head to smile at Colin again, she found him watching her, the brush he was cleaning held idly in one hand. Something pulled at her, urging her to go to him. Instead, she walked to the other end of the room.

"The first painting of yours I ever saw was an Irish landscape." Cassidy kept her back to him and tried to speak naturally. "It was a small, exquisite work bathed in evening light. I liked it because it helped me imagine my mother. Isn't that odd?" She turned back to him as the thought eclipsed her nerves. "I have several pictures of her, but that painting made her seem real. She rarely seems real to me." Her voice softened with the words; then, suddenly, she smiled at him. "Are your parents alive, Colin?"

His eyes held hers for a moment. "Yes." He went back to cleaning his brushes. "Back in Ireland."

"They must miss you."

"Perhaps. They've six other children. I don't imagine they find much time to be lonely."

"Six!" Cassidy exclaimed. Her lips curved at the thought. "Your mother must be remarkable."

Colin looked over again, flashing a grin. "She had a razor strap that could catch three of us at one time."

"No doubt you deserved it."

"No doubt." He scrutinized the sable of his brush. "But I recall wishing a time or two her aim hadn't been so keen."

"My father lectured," Cassidy remembered, taking a long breath in and out. "I'd often wish he'd whack me a time or two and be done with it. Lectures are a great deal more painful, I think, than a razor strap."

"Like Professor Easterman's at Berkeley?" Colin asked with a grin. Cassidy blinked at him.

"How did you know about him?"

"You told me yourself, Cass my love. Last week, I think it was. Or perhaps the week before."

"I never thought you were listening," she murmured. Cassidy tried to remember all she had rambled about since the sittings had begun. Her teeth began to worry her bottom lip. "I can't think of half the things I talked about."

"That's all right, I do . . . well enough." After wiping his hands on a rag, Colin turned back to her. She was frowning, displeased. "You've got those lines between your brows again, Cass," he said lightly and smiled when she smoothed them out. "Well now, I've made you miss lunch, and that's a crime when you're already thin enough to slip under the door. Shall I poison you with whatever's in the kitchen, or will you settle for coffee?"

"I think I'll pass on both those gracious invitations." She swung around and glided toward the dressing room. "I'll take my chances at home. I have a neighbor who hoards stale doughnuts."

Cassidy closed the door behind her and smiled. That wasn't so bad, she told her reflection. The ground was only shaky a couple of times. Now that the worst of it's over, the rest of the sittings should be easy.

Humming lightly, she began to strip out of the gown. Everything's going to be all right. After all, I'm a grown woman. I can handle myself.

After she had slipped out of the dress, Cassidy held it aloft to shake out the folds.

When the door opened, her humming turned to a shriek. In a quick jerk she pressed the dress against her naked skin and held on with both hands.

"What about dinner?" Colin asked and leaned against the open door.

"*Colin!*"

"Yes?" he asked in a pleasant tone.

"Colin, go away. I'm not dressed." She hugged the dress close and hoped she was somewhat covered.

"Yes, so I see, but you haven't answered my question."

Cassidy made an anxious sound and swallowed. "What question?"

"What about dinner?" he repeated. His eyes skimmed over her bare shoulders.

"*What* about dinner?" she demanded.

"You can't eat stale doughnuts for dinner, Cass. It's not healthy." He smiled at the incredulity on her face. She shifted the dress a bit higher.

"He keeps tacos as well," she said primly. "Now, would you mind shutting the door on your way out?"

"Tacos? Oh, no, that won't do." Colin shook his head and ignored her request. "I'll have to feed you myself."

Cassidy began to demand her privacy again then stopped. For a moment she studied him thoughtfully. "Colin, are you asking me for a date?"

"A date?" he repeated. For a moment he said nothing as he appeared to consider the matter. One brow arched as he studied her. "It certainly seems that way."

"To dinner?" Cassidy asked cautiously.

"To dinner."

"What time?"

"Seven."

"Seven," she repeated with a nod as she shut her ears on her practical side. "Now, close the door so I can get dressed."

"Certainly." A wicked gleam shot into his eyes, making her clutch the dress with both hands. She took one wary step in retreat. "By the way, Cass, you'd never've been a successful general."

"What?"

"You forgot to cover your flank," he told her as he shut the door behind him.

Twisting her head, Cassidy caught the full rear length of herself in the mirror.

Chapter 7

As Cassidy dressed that evening she blessed her short skip into the boutique business. The wisteria crepe de chine was worth all the hours she had practiced patience. It was a thin, dreamlike dress with floating lines. Her shoulders were left bare as the bodice was caught with elastic just above her breasts. The material nipped in at the waist then fell fully to the knees. She slipped on the cap-sleeved matching jacket and tied it loosely at the waist. The color was good for her eyes, she decided, bringing out the uniqueness of their shade. This was a night she didn't want to feel ordinary.

You shouldn't even be going. Cassidy brought the brush through her hair violently in response to the nagging voice. I don't care. I am going. *You'll get hurt.* I'll be hurt in any case. Moving quickly, she fastened small gold lover's knots to her ears. Doesn't everyone deserve one special moment? Aren't I entitled to a glimpse of real happiness? I'll have my one evening with him without that blasted painting between us. I'll have my moment when he's looking at me, seeing me, and not whatever it is he sees when we're in the studio.

She lifted her scent and sprayed a cloud as delicate as the wisteria. I won't think about tomorrow, only tonight. The painting's almost finished and then it'll be over. I have to have something. One evening isn't too much to ask. I'll pay the price later, but I'm going to have it. After tossing her hair behind her shoulders, Cassidy glanced at her watch.

"Oh, good grief, it's already seven!" Frantically she began to search for her key. She was on her hands and knees, peering under the convertible sofa that doubled as her bed, when the knock came. "Yes, yes, yes, just a minute," she called out crossly and stretched out for something shiny in the dark beneath the sofa.

She pulled it out with an "Aha!" of triumph, then sighed when she saw a quarter and not a key in her fingers.

"I said I'd buy," Colin told her, and Cassidy's head shot up. He stood inside her door, looking curiously at the woman on her hands and knees. Cassidy straightened up, blew her hair from her eyes and studied him.

He wore a slimly tailored black suit. Its

perfect cut accentuated the width of his shoulders and leanness of his build. His shirt was a splash of white in contrast and opened at the throat. Cassidy concluded Colin Sullivan would never restrict himself with a tie. She leaned back on her heels.

"I've never seen you in a suit before," she commented. The lamplight fell softly on her upturned face. "But you don't look too conventional. I'm glad."

"You're an amazing creature, Cassidy." He held out a hand to help her up, touching the other to her hair as she rose.

Standing, she tilted her head back and smiled at him. "Do you think so?"

A smile was his answer as he stepped back, keeping her hand in his. "You look lovely." The survey he made was quick and thorough. "Perfectly lovely." Taking her other hand, he turned it palm up and revealed the quarter. "Cab fare?" he asked. "It won't take you far."

Cassidy frowned down at her own hand. "I thought it was my key."

"Of course." Colin took the quarter and examined it critically. "It looks remarkably like one."

"It did in the dark under the sofa," Cassidy retorted then resumed her search. "It has to be here somewhere," she muttered as she shuffled through papers on her desk. "I've looked everywhere, positively everywhere."

"Where's the bedroom?" Colin asked, watching her shake out the pages of a dictionary.

"This *is* the bedroom," Cassidy informed him and poked through the leaves of a fern. "And the living room, and the study and the parlor. I like things all in one place, it saves steps." She found an eraser under a pile of notebooks and scowled at it. "I looked all over for this yesterday." With a long sigh she set it down.

"All right, just a minute," she said to the room in general as she leaned back on the desk. "I'll get it." Her eyes closed as she rubbed the tip of her finger over the bridge of her nose. "Last time I had it, I'd been to the market. I came in," she said, pointing to the door, "and I took the bag into the kitchen. I put a can of juice into the freezer, and . . ." Her eyes widened before she scrambled into the next room.

When she came back, she bounced the key from palm to palm. "It's cold," she explained and flushed under Colin's amused glance. "I must have been thinking of something else when I left it in there." Picking up a small gold bag, Cassidy dropped the frozen key inside. "That should do it." She moved to the door and engaged the lock. Gravely, Colin walked to her then cupped her face in his hands.

"Cass."

"Yes?"

"You don't have any shoes on."

"Oh." She lifted her shoulders then let them fall. "I suppose I'll need them."

He kissed her forehead and let her go. "It's best to be prepared for anything." A grin accompanied the gesture of his arm. "They seem to be by your desk."

In silence, Cassidy walked to the desk and slipped into her shoes. Her eyes were smiling as she returned to Colin. "Well, have I forgotten anything else?"

He took her hand, interlocking their fingers. "No."

"Do you like organized people particularly, Colin?" She tilted her head with the question.

"Not particularly."

"Good. Shall we go?"

Cassidy's first surprise of the evening was the Ferrari that sat by the curb. It was red and sleek and flashy. "That must be yours," she murmured, taking her eyes from bumper to bumper then back again.

"Or my neighbor has suddenly inherited a fortune."

"One of Vince's bribes." Colin opened the door on the passenger side. "For this I did a portrait of his niece. A remarkably plain creature with an overbite. Shall I put the top up?"

"No, don't." Cassidy settled into the seat as she watched him round the hood. Cinderella never had a pumpkin like this, she thought and smiled. "I thought you didn't paint anyone unless you were particularly interested in the subject."

"Vince is one of the few people I have difficulty refusing." The Ferrari roared into life. Excitement vibrated under Cassidy's feet.

"Did you know you can buy a three-bedroom brick rambler in New Jersey for what this car costs? With a carport and five spreading junipers."

Colin grinned and swung away from the curb. "I'd make a lousy neighbor."

Colin drove expertly through the city. They skirted Golden Gate Park, and avoided the labyrinthine stretches of freeway. They took side roads, narrow roads, and he maneuvered through traffic with smooth skill.

Cassidy could smell the varied scents from the sidewalk flower vendors and hear the brassy clang of the trolley bell. Tilting her head back, she could see the peak of a slender skyscraper. "Where're we going?" she asked but cared little as the breeze fluttered over her cheeks. It was enough to be with him.

"To eat," Colin returned. "I'm starving."

Cassidy turned to face him. "For an Irishman, you're not exactly talkative. Look." She sat up and pointed. "The fog's coming in."

It loomed over the bay, swallowing the bridge with surprising speed. As Cassidy watched, only the pinnacles of the Golden Gate speared the tumbling cloud.

"There'll be foghorns tonight," she murmured then looked at Colin again. "They make such a lonely sound. It always makes me sad, though I never know why."

"What sound makes you happy?" He glanced over to her, and she brushed wisps of flying hair from her face.

"Popping corn," she answered instantly then laughed at herself.

Leaning her head back, Cassidy looked up at the sky. It was piercingly blue. How many cities could have tumbling fog and blue skies? she wondered. When Colin pulled to the curb, her gaze traveled down until it encountered the huge expanse of the hotel. Her lips parted in surprise as she recognized the area. Nob Hill. She had paid no attention to their direction.

Her door was opened by a uniformed doorman who offered his hand to help her alight. She waited while Colin passed him a bill then joined her.

"Do you like seafood?" He took her hand and moved toward the entrance.

"Why, yes, I —"

"Good. They have rather exceptional seafood here."

"So I've heard," Cassidy murmured.

In a few steps she walked from a world she knew into one she had only read of.

The restaurant was huge and sumptuous. High, iridescent glass ceilings crowned a room dripping with chandeliers. The carpet was rich, the tables many and elegantly white clothed. The maître d' was immediately attentive, and as Colin called him by name Cassidy realized the artist was no stranger there.

The secluded corner table set them apart from the vastness of the restaurant yet left Cassidy with a full view of the splendor. Jeff's cheeseburger seemed light-years away. Having gawked as much as she deemed proper, Cassidy turned to Colin.

"It seems I'm going to do better than tacos after all."

"I'm a man of my word," he informed her. "That's why I give it as seldom as possible. Wine?" he asked and smiled at her in his masterfully charming fashion. "You don't look the cocktail type."

"Oh?" Her head tilted. "Why not?"

"Too much innocence in those big violet eyes." He brushed her hair behind her shoulder. "It almost makes me consider doing something bourgeois like cutting the wine with water."

A black-coated waiter stood respectfully at Colin's elbow. "A bottle of Château Haut-Brion blanc," he ordered, keeping his eyes on Cassidy. With a slight bow the waiter drifted backward and away. She watched him then took another long look around the room, trying to absorb every detail. "I noticed by your desk that you've been working. Is it going well?"

Cassidy studied Colin with some surprise. Perhaps he saw more than she assumed he did. "Yes, actually, I think it is. I'm having one of those periods when everything falls into place. They don't last long, but they're productive. Does it work like that with painting?"

"Yes. Times when everything seems to

flow without effort, and times when you scrape the canvas down again and again." He smiled at her, and his long fingers traced her wrist. "Somewhat like you tearing up pages, I imagine."

The waiter returned with their wine, and the ritual of opening and tasting began. Gratefully, Cassidy remained silent. The pulse in her wrist had leapt at Colin's casual touch, and she used the time to quiet its skittish rhythm. When her glass was filled, she was able to lift it with complete composure. The wine was lightly chilled and exquisite.

"To your taste?" Colin asked as he watched her sip.

Cassidy's eyes smiled into his. "It could become a habit."

"Tell me what you're writing about." He, too, lifted his glass, but his free hand covered hers.

"It's about two people and their life together and apart from each other."

"A love story?"

"Yes, a complex one." She frowned a moment at their joined hands then brought her eyes to Colin's again. The flame of the candle threw gold among the violet. She reminded herself to enjoy the moment, not to think of tomorrow. A smile lifted her lips as she touched the glass to them. "They both seem to be volatile characters and get away from me sometimes. There's a fierce determination in them both to stand separate, yet they're drawn together. I'd like to think love allows them to remain separate in some aspects."

"Love makes its own rules, depending on who's playing." His finger trailed over her knuckles then down to her nails before they traveled back. The simple gesture quickened her heartbeat. "Will they have a happy ending?"

Cassidy allowed herself to absorb the pure blue of his eyes. "Perhaps they will," she murmured. "Their destinies are in my hands."

Watching her, Colin brought her hand to his lips. "And for tonight, Cass," he said softly, "is yours in mine?"

Her eyes were dark and steady on his. "For tonight."

He smiled then, with the flash of the pirate. Lifting his glass, he toasted her. "To the long evening ahead."

It was a luxuriously lengthy meal. Wine sparkled in crystal. Even after endless courses, they lingered long over coffee. Cassidy savored each moment. If she was to have only one evening with the man she loved, she would relish each morsel of time. Perhaps by the force of her own will, she could slow the hands of the clock.

The candle flickered low when they rose from the table. Her hand slipped into his. Just as they reached the lobby Cassidy heard Colin's name called. Looking up, she saw a round, balding man in an impeccably cut suit coming toward them. He had a full smile and an extended hand. On reaching Colin, he pumped it enthusiastically while his other thumped on Colin's shoulder. Cassidy saw a large diamond flash from the ring on his hand.

"Sullivan, you rascal, it's good to see you."

"Jack." An easy grin spread over Colin's face. "How've you been?"

"Getting by, getting by. Have a little job in town." His eyes drifted to Cassidy and lingered.

"Cass, this is Jack Swanson, a perfect reprobate. Jack, Cassidy St. John, a perfect treasure."

Cassidy was torn between pleasure at Colin's description and astonishment as she put Swanson's face and name together. Over the past twenty-five years he had produced some of the finest motion pictures in the industry. As he took her hand and squeezed it, she struggled to conceal her feelings.

"Reprobate?" Swanson snorted and kept possession of Cassidy's hand. "You can't believe half the things this Irishman says. I'm a pillar of the community."

"There's a plaque in his den that says so," Colin added.

"Never did have an ounce of respect. Still . . ." Swanson's eyes roamed over Cassidy's face. There was appreciation in the look. "His taste is flawless. Not an actress, are you?"

"Not unless you count being a mushroom in the fourth-grade pageant." Cassidy smiled.

Swanson chuckled and nodded. "I've dealt with actresses who had lesser credits."

"Cassidy's a writer," Colin put in. He draped an arm around her shoulders, running his hand lightly down her arm. "You warned me to stay away from actresses."

"Since when have you listened to my sage advice?" Swanson scoffed. He pursed his lips as he studied Cassidy. Appreciation became speculation. "A writer. What sort of writer are you?"

"Why, a brilliant one, of course," she told him. "Without a scrap of ego or temperament."

Swanson patted her hand. "I've a late meeting or I'd steal you away from this young scamp now. We'll have dinner before I leave town." He cast an eye at Colin. "You can bring him along if you like." With another slap for Colin's shoulder, he lumbered away.

"Quite a character, isn't he?" Colin asked as he steered Cassidy toward the door again.

"Marvelous." It occurred to her that since meeting Colin, she had held hands with an Italian duke and one of Hollywood's reigning monarchs.

They stepped outside into the soft light of evening. The sun was gone, but some of its light still lingered. Cassidy slipped into the Ferrari with a contented sigh. She watched the first star flicker into life. With surprise she noted that Colin was headed away from the direction of her apartment.

"Where are we going?"

"There's this little place I know." He turned a corner and eased into traffic. "I thought you'd enjoy it." He shot her a glance and a smile. "Not tired, are you?"

Cassidy's lips curved. "No, I'm not tired."

The nightclub was dimly lit and smoky. Tables were small and crowded together.

Jeans sat next to elegant evening dresses and splashy designer outfits. Brassy music blared from a band near a postage-stamp dance floor. Couples swayed together as they moved to the beat.

Colin escorted Cassidy to a dark table at the side of the room. His name was called now and again, but he only made a gesture of acknowledgment and continued until they were seated.

"This is wonderful! I'm certain it's a front for gun running or jewel smuggling," Cassidy exclaimed.

Colin laughed, taking both her hands. "You'd like that, would you?"

"Of course." She grinned, and her eyes lit with mischief.

A waitress had pushed her way over to them and stood, impatient, with her weight on one hip. "The lady needs champagne," Colin told her.

"Who doesn't," she mumbled and shoved her way back through the tables.

Cassidy laughed with unbridled delight. "No deferential bows for Mr. Sullivan in here," she commented.

"It's all a matter of atmosphere. I'm rather fond of sassy waitresses in the right setting. And," he added softly, turning her hand over and kissing the inside of her wrist, "crowded tables that require very close contact. Poor lighting," he continued, pressing his lips to her palm. "Where I can enjoy the taste of your skin in relative privacy." With a slight movement of his head, he kissed the sensitive skin behind her ear.

"Colin," she said breathlessly and lifted her hand to his lips in defense. He merely took it in his and kissed her fingers.

The bottle of champagne came down on the table with a bang. Colin pulled out a bill and handed it to the waitress. Shoving it in her pocket, she stalked away.

"Annoyingly speedy service tonight," he murmured as he opened the bottle. The pop was drowned out by the loud horns of the band. Cassidy accepted the wine and took a long, slow sip in the hope of stabilizing her pulse.

They drank champagne in quiet companionship, watching the raucous nightlife revolve around them. Cassidy's mood grew mellow and dreamy. Reality and make-believe became too difficult to separate. When Colin stood and took her hand, she rose to go with him to the dance floor.

The music had turned low and bluesy. He slipped both arms around her waist, and in response she lifted hers to circle his neck. Their bodies came together. The air was thick with smoke and clashing perfumes. Other couples were little more than shadows in the dim light. Their movement was only a slow swaying with their bodies pressed close.

Cassidy tilted back her head to look at him. Their eyes joined, their lips tarried less than a whisper apart. She felt a quick surge of desire. If they had been on an island without a trace of humanity, she could not have felt more alone with him. The music ended on a haunted bass note.

Silently Colin took her hand and led her from the crowd.

The moon was a white slice. Cooler air blew some of the heat from Cassidy's blood and some of the clouds from her brain. The Ferrari climbed a hill then descended. Cassidy smiled to herself. There was nothing in the evening she would have changed. No regrets.

Fog curled in twisting fingers on the road ahead. As she glanced to the side Cassidy saw the solid mass of clouds over the bay below them. Again she turned to Colin.

"To my houseboat," he told her before she could form the question. "I have something for you."

Warning lights flashed on and off in her brain. The bittersweet taste of danger was in her mouth. Cassidy looked out on the fog-choked bay and told herself she should ask Colin to take her home. But the night isn't over, she reminded herself. I promised myself tonight.

Fog swirled more thickly as they drove toward sea level. Now and again, from somewhere deep in the mist, came the low warning horns. She'd lost all sense of time when Colin stopped the car. Once again she was in a make-believe world. This one had drifting mists and the sigh of lapping water. Colin led her toward a shrouded shape. The high, maniacal call of a loon speared the silence. A narrow rope bridge swayed lightly under her feet as they crossed it. A breeze blew aside a curtain of fog, and the houseboat jumped into the opening.

"Oh, Colin." She stopped to stare at it with delight and surprise. "It's wonderful."

She saw a wide structure of aged wood in two levels with a high deck on the bow. Fog misted over again as they approached.

Inside Cassidy shook the dampness from her hair as Colin switched on a light. They walked down two steps and into the living room. It was a large square room with a low, inviting couch and tables scattered for convenience. To the right another short set of stairs led to the galley.

"How marvelous to live on the water." Cassidy spun to Colin and smiled.

"On a clear night the city's all prisms and crystals. In the fog it's brooding and wrapped in mystery." He came to her and, with a habitual gesture, brushed her hair behind her shoulder. His fingers lingered. "Your hair's damp," he murmured. "Do you know how many shades of gold and brown I used to paint your hair? It changes in every light, daring someone to define its color." Colin frowned suddenly and dropped his hand. "You should have a brandy to ward off the chill."

He turned away and walked to a cabinet. Cassidy watched him pour brandy into snifters while she dealt with the effect the intimate tone of his voice and the touch of his hand had had on her.

After accepting the brandy she turned to wander around the room. On a far wall was a painting of the bay at sunrise. The sky was molten with color, reds and golds at their most intense. There was a feeling of frenzied motion and brilliance. Even before she looked for the signature, Cassidy knew it was a Kingsley.

"She's immensely talented," Colin commented from behind.

"Yes," Cassidy agreed with sincerity. The painting gripped her. "It makes the start of a day demand your attention. A sunrise like this would be exciting, but I don't think I could begin each morning with such violence, however beautiful."

"Are you speaking of the painting or of the artist?"

Realizing his question had followed her thoughts, Cassidy shrugged and stepped away. "Strange," she began again. "One would think an artist would cover his walls with paintings. You have relatively few." She began to examine his collection, moving slowly from one to the next. Abruptly she stopped, staring at a small canvas. It was the Irish landscape she had told him of that morning.

"I wondered if you'd remember it." He stood behind her again, but this time his hands came to her shoulders. There was something casually possessive in the gesture.

"Yes, of course I do."

"I was twenty when I painted that. On my first trip back to Ireland."

"How odd that I should have spoken of it just this morning," Cassidy murmured.

"Destiny, Cass," Colin claimed and kissed the top of her head. Stepping around her, he took the canvas from the wall. "I want you to have it."

Cassidy's eyes flew to his. "No, Colin, I couldn't." Distress and amazement mingled in her voice.

"No?" His brow arched under his fall of hair. "You appeared to like it."

"Oh, Colin, you know I do. It's beautiful, it's wonderful." Her distress deepened, reflecting clearly on her face. "I can't just take one of your paintings."

"You're not taking it, I'm giving it to you," he countered. "That's one of the privileges of the artist."

"Colin." Her eyes went back to the painting then lifted to his. "You wouldn't have kept it all this time if it hadn't meant something special to you. You'd have sold it."

"Some things you don't sell. Some things you give." He held the small canvas out to her. "Please."

Tears thickened in her throat. "I've never heard you say 'please' before."

"I save it for special occasions."

Cassidy looked back at him. He had given her more than the painting; it was a bond — between herself and a woman she had never known. Her smile came slowly. "Thank you."

Colin traced her lips with a fingertip. "This is one of the loveliest things about you," he murmured. "Come," he said abruptly. "Sit down and drink your brandy." He took the canvas and set it aside, then led Cassidy to the sofa.

"Do you paint here, too?" she asked as she sipped her brandy.

"Sometimes."

"I remember the night I met you, your wanting me to come back here for sketches."

"And you threatened me with a husband in a football helmet."

"It was the best I could think up on the spur of the moment." She turned her head to grin at him and found his face dangerously close. His fingers tangled in her hair before she could ease away. Slowly he leaned closer until his lips brushed her cheek. Feather light, the kiss moved to her other cheek, lingering over her lips without touching. Still, she could taste the kiss on them.

"Colin," Cassidy whispered. She put a hand to his chest as his lips moved to her temple. She knew the warmth she felt was not from the brandy.

"Cassidy." He trailed his mouth down to her jawline then drew away. His eyes were grave as he looked down at her, his hand light on her shoulder. "The last time I kissed you, I hurt you. I regret that."

"Please, Colin." Cassidy shook her head to halt his words. "We were both angry."

"You've already forgiven me, because it's your nature to do so. But I remember the look on your face." He ran his hand down her arm until it linked with hers. "I want to kiss you again, Cass, the way you should be kissed." He took his hand and gently circled her neck. "But I need you to tell me it's what you want."

It would be so easy to refuse. She had only to form the word "no," and she knew he'd let her go. But she was as truly his prisoner now as if she were chained to him. "Yes," she said and closed her eyes. "Yes."

His mouth touched hers lightly, and her lips parted. His kisses were soft and gentle, lingering before one ended and another began. She felt him slip the light jacket from her shoulders and enjoyed the warmth of his hands on her skin. Slowly the kisses grew deeper. Her arms found their way around him. The languor that spread through her went far beyond the effects of the wine. Her limbs were pliant, her mind clouded as her senses grew sharper.

When their lips parted, Colin loosened his hold. "Cass."

With a sigh she snuggled against him, brushing his neck with a kiss. She ran a hand experimentally up the silk of his shirt. "Yes?" she murmured, lifting her face to his. Her eyes were slumberous, her lips a temptation. Colin swore under his breath before he crushed his mouth to hers.

Cassidy's response was instantaneous. Her passion went from languid to flaming in the space of a heartbeat. Blood pounded thickly in her brain as she found herself falling backward onto the cushions of the sofa. Colin's body was taut. His hands caressed the bare skin of her shoulders as the kiss deepened. At the base of her throat he found more pleasure, and his mouth lingered there as her pulse beat wildly beneath it.

The elastic of her bodice slid down at his insistence, freeing her breasts to his searching hands. Unbridled, her passion raced through her, bringing a moan that spoke of longing and delight. His mouth trailed down through the valley between her breasts, devouring her heated skin. His fingers brushed over the peak of her breasts, exploring, learning, until his mouth replaced them. Cassidy gave a shuddering moan as he brought his lips back to hers, accepting the fierce, final urgency that flared before he ended the kiss. Her eyes opened to meet the dark fire of his.

Seeing the tumble of his hair over his brow, she lifted a hand to push it back. She murmured his name. Colin caught her hand in his as she took it to his cheek. Carefully he drew the bodice of her dress into place then pulled her with him to a sitting position.

"I make few noble gestures, Cassidy." His voice was husky, and under her palm she could feel the rapid beat of his heart. "This is one of them." Rising, he drew her to her feet then draped her jacket over her shoulders. "I'll take you home."

"Colin," she began, knowing only that she wanted to be his.

"No, don't say anything." He dropped his hands from her shoulders and put them in his pockets. "You put your destiny in my hands for tonight. I'll take you home. Next time the decision will be in your hands."

Chapter 8

The sun was high and bright. Cassidy watched it spear through her window as she lay in bed. It fell in a patch on the floor and shimmered. Her eyes drifted to the painting that hung to her left. It had hung there for only two days, but she knew every minute detail of the canvas. She knew the very texture of the brush strokes. Sighing, she stared up at the ceiling.

She remembered every moment of her evening with Colin, from the instant she had looked up from her hands and knees by her couch to the brief good-bye at the door.

When she had returned to the studio the morning after their date, Colin had fallen into his work pattern with apparent ease. Whatever had been between them, Cassidy decided, had been for that night. For him, it was over. For me, she thought, studying the painting again, it's forever.

I should be grateful to him for taking me home when he did. If I had stayed . . . If I had stayed, she repeated after a long breath, I would have become one of his lovers. And then he would have picked up his life exactly where he left off, and I would be even more alone than I am now. As it is, I have one exceptional evening to remember. Wine and candlelight and music.

"Romantic fool," she muttered abruptly then rolled over and punched her pillow.

"Cassidy." The knock sounded as a brief concession before Jeff burst through the door. "Hey, Cassidy." He stopped and gave her a look of disgust. "Still in bed? It's eleven o'clock."

Cassidy pulled the sheet up to her chin and scrambled to sit up. "Yes, I'm still in bed. I worked till three-thirty." She frowned past him. "I thought I'd remembered to lock that door."

"Uh-uh." Jeff hurried over and plopped on the bed while she flushed with embarrassed amusement.

"Make yourself at home," she said with a grand gesture of her free arm. "Don't mind me."

"Take a look at this! You got yourself in the paper."

"What?" Cassidy glanced down at the newspaper Jeff had clutched in his hand. "What are you talking about?"

"I splurged on a Sunday paper," he began then his lips spread in a grin. He touched her nose with a fingertip. "And who do I see when I take a look at the society section, but my friend and neighbor, Cassidy St. John."

"You're making that up," Cassidy accused and tossed back her sleep-tumbled hair. "What would I be doing on the society page?"

"Dancing with Colin Sullivan," Jeff informed her as he waved the paper under her nose.

Cassidy grabbed his wrist to stop the movement, then her mouth fell open in astonishment. She stared, unbelievingly, at the picture. In two quick moves she had dropped the sheet and grabbed the paper from Jeff's hand. "Let me see that."

"Help yourself," he said amiably. He settled back on one elbow to watch myriad expressions cross her face. The flush sleep had put into her cheeks grew deeper. "Seems you were seen together in some hot spot. A picture gets snapped, and they add a bit of interesting speculation of who Sullivan's latest flame is." He pulled on his beard and chuckled. "Little do they know she's sitting right here in a number fifty-three football jersey that looks a lot better

158

on her than it would on a right tackle." He chuckled again then peered down at the newspaper. "You look real good in there, too."

"This is all — all drivel!" Cassidy slammed down the paper then scrambled to her knees. Pushing Jeff aside she stepped over him to the floor. "Did you read that story?" she demanded and kicked a stray tennis shoe into a corner. "How dare they imply such things?"

Jeff sat back up, watching her spin around the room. "Hey, Cassidy, it's just a story, nothing to get all worked up about. Besides . . ." He picked up the discarded paper and smoothed it out. "They're really pretty complimentary where you're concerned. Listen, they call you a . . ." He paused while he searched down the phrase. "Oh, yeah, here it is. A 'nubile young beauty.' Sounds pretty good."

Cassidy made a low sound in her throat then kicked the mate to the tennis shoe into an opposing corner. "That's just like a man," she stormed back at him. Turning away, she pulled open a drawer and yanked out a pair of cutoffs; then, spinning around, she waved them at him. "Toss out a few compliments and it makes everything all right." Cassidy dove back into the drawer and came up with a crimson scoop-necked T-shirt. "Well, it's not, it's absolutely not." She pushed her hair out of her face and drew in a deep breath. "Can I keep that?" she asked in more controlled tones.

"Sure." Warily, Jeff rose and handed her the paper. He cleared his throat. "Well, I guess I'll just go read the rest of the paper," he told her, but she was already scowling down at the picture again. Taking advantage of her preoccupation, he slipped out the door.

Less than an hour later Cassidy was stalking down the pier toward Colin's houseboat. Gripped in her hand was the folded page of the Sunday paper. Filled with righteous indignation, she crossed the narrow swaying bridge then pounded on the door. There was silence and the lapping of waves. She glanced around then scowled at the Ferrari.

"Oh, you're home all right, Sullivan," she muttered darkly then pounded again.

"What the devil are you banging about?" Colin's voice boomed over her head. Cassidy backed away from the door, looked up and was blinded by the sun. Furious, she flung up a hand to shade her eyes.

She saw him leaning over the rail of the top deck. He was bare-chested, his cutoffs a slight concession to modesty. He held a paint brush tipped in blue in his hand.

"I've got to talk to you!" Cassidy shouted and waved the paper at him.

"All right then, come up, but stop that idiotic banging." He disappeared from the rail before she could speak again. Cassidy walked toward the bow until she spotted a steep set of stairs. After climbing them, she stood on the upper deck with her hands on her hips. She scowled at his back.

He was on a three-legged stool in front of a canvas, painting with sure, rapid strokes. Glancing over, she saw the sailboats he was recreating. They skimmed over the bay with spinnakers billowing in a riot of color.

"Well, what brings you rapping at my door, Cass?" His voice was muffled as he held the stem of a brush between his teeth like a pirate's saber. Another glided over the canvas. Cassidy stomped over and fearlessly waved the paper in front of his face.

"This!"

With surprising calm, Colin put down both of his brushes, cast her a raised-brow look, then took the paper from her. "It's a good likeness," he said after a moment.

"*Colin!*"

"Ssh. I'm reading." He lapsed into silence, eyes on the paper, while Cassidy ground her teeth and stalked around the deck. Once he laughed outright but held up a hand when she started to speak. She shut her mouth on something like a growl and turned her back on him. "Well," he said at length. "That was highly entertaining."

Cassidy whirled around. "Entertaining? *Entertaining?!* Is that all you have to say about this — this trash?"

Colin shrugged. "It could be better written, I suppose. Do you want coffee?"

"Did you *read* that?" she demanded and stormed forward until she stood in front of him. The wind tugged at her hair, and she pushed it back, annoyed. "Did you read the things it said, the things . . ." Cassidy sputtered to a halt, stomped her foot in frustration then gave him a firm rap on the chest with her fist. "I am not your latest flame, Sullivan."

"Ah."

Her eyes kindled. "Don't you use that significant 'ah' on me. I am *not* your latest flame, or your flame of any sort, and I resent the term. I resent all the little insinuations

162

and innuendos in that article. I resent the unstated fact that you and I are lovers." She tossed back her head. "What sort of logic is it that because we dance together, we have to be lovers?"

"You have to admit the idea is appealing." He chuckled at her smoldering glare. The breeze rolling in from the bay continued to blow her hair around her face. Absently Colin brushed it back then laid a hand on her shoulder. "Would you like to sue the paper?"

She heard the soft amusement in his voice and stuck her hands in her pockets. "I want a retraction," she said stubbornly.

"For what?" he countered. "For snapping a picture? For writing a bit of gossip? My dear child, the picture's enough all by itself." He held it out, drawing her eyes to it. "These two people appear to be totally absorbed in each other."

Cassidy turned away and walked to the rail. She knew it had been the picture that had set her off. Their bodies were close, her arms around his neck, their eyes locked. The dark, smoky nightclub was a backdrop. No words were needed to complete the picture. She remembered the moment, the feeling that had rushed through her, the utter intimacy they had shared.

The picture was an invasion of her private self, and she hated it. She detested the chatty little column beside it that linked her so casually with Colin. Without even having learned her name, they had titled her his woman, his woman of the moment . . . until the next one. Cassidy frowned out at the water, watching the gulls swoop.

"I don't like it," she muttered. "I don't like being splashed in print for speculation over cornflakes and coffee. I don't like being made into something I'm not by someone's lively imagination. And I don't like being described as a . . ."

" 'Nubile young beauty'?" Colin provided.

"I see nothing funny in that grand little phrase. It makes me feel absurd." She folded her arms over her chest. "It's not a compliment, whatever you and Jeff might think."

"Who the devil is Jeff?"

"He thought the article was just peachy," she continued, working up to a high temper again. "He sat on my bed this morning, telling me I should be flattered, that I should —"

"Perhaps," Colin interrupted and walked to her, "you'd tell me who Jeff is and why he was in your bed this morning?"

"Not in, *on*," Cassidy corrected impatiently. "And stick to the point, Sullivan."

"I'd like this matter cleared up first." He took a final step toward her then captured her chin. His fingers were surprisingly firm. "In fact, I insist."

"Will you stop it?" she demanded and jerked away. "How can I get anywhere when you're constantly badgering and belittling me."

"Badgering and belittling?" Colin repeated then tossed back his head and roared with laughter. "Now *that's* a grand little phrase. Now, about Jeff."

"Oh, leave him out of it, would you?" Cassidy blew out a frustrated breath, making a wide sweep with her arms. Her eyes began to glitter again. "He brought me the article this morning, that's all. I'm telling you, Colin, I won't be lumped in with all your former and future flames. And I won't be used to sustain the romantic mystique of the artist."

His brows drew together. "Now what precisely is the meaning of that last sentence, for those of us who missed the first installment?"

"I think it's clear, a simple declarative sentence in the first person. I mean it, Colin."

"Yes." He studied her curiously. "I can see you do."

They watched each other in silence. She was painfully aware of the lean attraction of his build, of the bronzed skin left bare but for low-slung cutoffs. Thrown off balance by her own thoughts, Cassidy turned away again and leaned over the rail. For a moment she listened to the gentle slap of water against the wood of the boat. Her shoulders moved with her sigh.

"I'm basically a simple person, Colin. I've never been out of the state and scarcely been more than a hundred miles from the city. I don't have a fascinating background. I'm not a woman of mystery." Composed again, she turned back to him. The breeze picked up her hair and tossed it behind her. "I don't like being misrepresented." She lifted her hands a moment then dropped them to her sides. "I'm not the sort of woman they made me seem in that paper."

Colin folded the paper then tucked it in his back pocket before he crossed to her. "You are infinitely more fascinating than the sort of woman they made you seem in that paper."

Cassidy shook her head. "I wasn't fishing for a compliment."

"A simple statement of fact." He kissed

her before she could decide whether to accept or evade him. "Feel better now?"

Cassidy frowned at him. "I'm not a child having a temper tantrum."

His brow lifted. "A nubile young beauty, then."

Cassidy narrowed her eyes at him then glanced down at herself. "I'm nubile enough, I should think."

"And certainly young."

Bringing her eyes back up, she gave him a provocative look. "Don't you think I'm beautiful?"

"No."

"Oh."

Colin laughed then captured her face with his hands. "That face," he said as his eyes roamed over her, "has superb bones, exquisite skin. There's strength and frailty and vivacity, and you're totally unaware of it. A unique, expressive face. Beautiful is far too ordinary a word."

Color warmed Cassidy's cheeks. She wondered why, after so many close examinations, her blood still churned when he studied her face. "A charming way to make up for an insult," she said lightly. "It must be the Irish in you."

"I've a much better way."

The kiss was so quickly insistent, Cassidy

had no time for thought, only response. A sound of pleasure escaped her as she moved her hands up the taut, bare skin of his chest. She felt the heat of the sun and her own instant need. Her mouth became avid. Desire swirled through her blood, causing her to demand rather than surrender. The passion he released in her ruled her, changing submission to aggression. She felt Colin's arms tighten around her and heard his low moan of approval.

"Cassidy," he murmured as his lips roamed over her face. "You bewitch me."

With a curiosity of their own, her hands explored the long line of his torso, the wiry muscles of his arms and back. His heart hammered against hers as she touched him. Here was a whole new world, and her mouth searched his ravenously as she tested it.

"Oh, dear, I seem to be interrupting."

Startled, Cassidy pulled her mouth from Colin's but was unable to break his hold. Twisting her head, she stared at Gail Kingsley. She stood just at the top of the stairs, one hand poised on the railing. An emerald silk scarf rippled at her throat and trailed in the breeze.

"That seems obvious enough," Colin returned evenly. Flushing to the roots of her hair, Cassidy wriggled for freedom.

"I do apologize, Colin darling. I had no idea you had company. So rare for you on a Sunday, after all." She gave him a smile that established her knowledge of his habits. "I needed to pick up those Rothchild canvases, you remember? And we do have one or two things to discuss. I'll just wait downstairs." She crossed the deck as she spoke and opened a door that led inside. "Shall I make coffee for three?" she added then disappeared without waiting for an answer.

Cassidy twisted her head back to Colin, pressing her hands against his chest. "Let me go," she demanded between her teeth. "Let me go this minute."

"Why? You seemed happy enough to be held a moment ago."

She threw back her head as she shoved against him. The muscles she had just tested made her movements useless. "A moment ago I was blinded by animal lust. I see perfectly now."

"Animal lust?" Colin repeated. He grinned widely in appreciation. "How interesting. Does it come over you often?"

"Don't you grin at me, Sullivan. Don't you dare!"

Colin released her without sobering his

features. "At times it's difficult not to."

"I won't have you holding me while Gail stands there with her superior little smile." With a sniff, she brushed at her T-shirt and shorts.

"Why, Cass, are you jealous?" His grin grew yet wider. "How flattering."

Her head snapped up, her breathing grew rapid. "Why you smug, insufferable —"

"You were perfectly willing to suffer me when you were blinded by animal lust."

A sound of temper came low in her throat. Tested past her limit, Cassidy took an enthusiastic swing at him that carried her in a complete circle. He dodged it, catching her neatly by the waist.

"Women are supposed to slap," he instructed. "Not punch."

"I never read the rules," she snapped then jerked away. Cassidy turned, intending to leave in the same manner she had arrived. Colin caught her hand and spun her back until she collided with his chest. He smiled then kissed the tip of her nose.

"What's your hurry?"

"There's an old Irish saying," she told him as she pushed away again. "Three's a crowd."

He chuckled, patting her cheek. "Cass, don't be a fool."

She rolled her eyes to the sky and prayed for willpower. Screaming wouldn't solve anything. She took several deep breaths. "Oh, go . . . go paint your spinnakers," she suggested and stalked down the steps to the lower deck.

"Sure and it's a fine-looking woman you are, Cassidy St. John," Colin called after her in an exaggerated brogue. She glanced back over her shoulder with eyes blazing. He leaned companionably over the rail. "And it's the truth it's no more hardship watching your temper walking away than it is watching it coming ahead. Next time I'll be wanting to paint you in a pose that shows your more charming end."

"When pigs fly," she called back and doubled her pace. His laughter raced after her.

Chapter 9

Cassidy knew the painting was nearly finished. She had the frantic, hollow sensation of one living on borrowed time. Though she sensed the end would be almost a relief, a release from the tension of waiting, she tried to hold it off by sheer force of will. As she held the pose, she sensed Colin was perfecting, polishing, rather than creating fresh. His quick impatience had relaxed.

He made no mention of her Sunday visit, and she was grateful. In retrospect, with her temper at a reasoning degree, she knew she had overreacted. She was also forced to admit that she had made a fool of herself. A complete fool.

It's not the first time, she mused. And perhaps, in a way, excusable. All I could see was a very public picture revealing my very private feelings. Then that silly little article . . . Then remembering Gail's spouting off about romantic press and Colin's image. Cassidy caught herself before she scowled. Well, I won't have to listen to her much longer. I'd better start picking up the pieces. It's time to start thinking about to-morrow. A new job, she concluded dis-mally. A new start, she corrected. New experiences, new people. Empty nights.

"Fortunately, I finished the face yes-terday," Colin commented. "Your expres-sion's altered a dozen times in the last ten minutes. Amazing what a range you have."

"I'm sorry. I was . . ." She searched for a word and settled on an inanity. "Thinking."

"Yes, I could see." His eyes caught hers. "Unhappy thoughts."

"No, I was working out a scene."

"Mmm," Colin commented non-committally then stepped back from the easel. "Not a particularly joyful one."

"No. They can't all be." She swallowed. "It's finished, isn't it?"

"Yes. Quite finished." Cassidy let out a quiet sigh as she watched his critical study. "Come, have a look," he invited. He held out his hand, but his eyes remained on the canvas.

It surprised her that she was afraid. Colin glanced up at her and lifted a brow.

"Come on, then."

Her fingers tightened around the nosegay, but she walked toward him. Obe-diently she slipped her hand into his ex-tended one. She turned and looked.

Cassidy had tried to imagine it a hundred times, but it was nothing like what she'd thought. The background was dark and shadowy, playing on shading and depth. In its midst, she stood highlighted in the oyster-white dress. Her nosegay was a surprising splash of color calling attention to the frailty of her hands. Pride was in the stance, in the tilt of her head. Her hair was thick and gloriously tumbled, offsetting the quiet innocence of the dress. It was hair that invited passion. There was a delicacy in the bones of her face she had been unaware of, a fragility competing with the strength of the features. She had been right in thinking he would see her as she had never seen herself.

Her lips were parted, unsmiling but waiting to smile. The smile would be to welcome a lover. The knowledge was in her expression, along with the anticipation of something yet to come. The eyes told everything. They were the eyes of a woman consumed by love . . . the eyes of innocence waiting to be surrendered. No one could look at it and remain unaware that the woman in the painting had loved the man who painted it.

"So silent, Cass?" Colin murmured and slipped an arm around her shoulders.

"I can't find the word," she whispered then drew a trembling breath. "Nothing's adequate, and anything less would sound platitudinous." She leaned against him a moment. "Colin." Cassidy tried to forget for a moment that the eyes in the painting were naked with love. She tried to see the whole and not the revelation of her emotions. Secrets, he had said. Dreams.

Colin kissed her neck above the silk of the dress then released her. "Rarely, an artist steps back from his work and is astonished that his hands have created something extraordinary." She could hear the excitement in his voice, a wonder she had not expected him to be capable of feeling. "This is the finest thing I've ever done." He turned to her then. "I'm grateful to you, Cassidy. You're the soul of it."

Unable to bear his words, Cassidy turned away. She had to cling to some rags of pride. Desperately she kept her voice calm. "I've always felt the artist is the soul of a painting." Cassidy dropped the nosegay on the worktable then continued to wander around the room. The silk whispered over her legs. "It's your — your imagination, your talent. How much of me is really in that painting?"

There was silence for a long moment,

but Cassidy didn't turn back to him. "Don't you know?" Cassidy moistened her lips and struggled to keep her tone light as she turned around.

"My face," she agreed; then, gesturing down the dress, she added, "My body. The rest is yours, Colin, I can't take credit for it. You set the mood, you drew out of me what you already saw. You had the vision. It was a wish you asked me to be, and that's what you've made. It's your illusion." Saying the words caused her more pain than she had believed possible. Still, she felt they had to be said.

"Is that how you see it?" Colin's look was speculative, but she sensed the anger just beneath the surface. "You stood, and I pulled the strings."

"You're the artist, Colin." She shrugged and answered lightly. "I'm just an unemployed writer."

After a long, silent study, he crossed to her. There was a steady calculation about the way his hands took her shoulders. She had felt that seeking, probing look before and stiffened her defenses against it. His fingers tightened on her skin. "Has the woman in that portrait anything to do with you?" He asked the question slowly.

Cassidy swallowed the knot in her

throat. "Why, of course, Colin, I've just told you —"

He shook her so quickly, the words slid back down her throat. She saw the fury on his face, the vivid temper she knew could turn violent. "Do you think it was only your face I wanted? Just the shell? Is there nothing that's inside you in that painting?"

"Must you have everything?" she demanded in despair and anger. "Must you have it all?" Her voice thickened with emotion. "You've drained me, Colin. That's drained me." She flung a hand toward the canvas. "I've given you everything, how much more do you want?"

She pushed him away as a tidal wave of anguish engulfed her. "You never looked at me, thought of me, unless it was because of that painting." She pushed her hair back with both hands, pressing her fingers against her temples. "I won't give you anymore. I can't, there isn't any. It's all there!" She gestured again, and her voice shook. "Thank God it's over."

With a quick jerk, she was out of his hold and running from the studio.

Cassidy spent the next two weeks in the apartment of vacationing friends. Leaving a brief note for Jeff, she packed up her typewriter and buried herself in work. She unplugged the phone, bolted the door and shut herself in. For two weeks she tried to forget there was a world outside the people and places of her imagination. She lost herself in her characters in an attempt to forget Cassidy St. John. If she didn't exist, she couldn't feel pain. At the end of the interlude, she'd shed five pounds, produced a hundred pages of fresh copy and nearly balanced her nerves.

As she returned, hauling her typewriter back up the steps to her apartment, she heard Jeff's guitar playing through his door. For a moment she hesitated, thinking to stop and tell him she was back, but she passed into her own apartment. She wasn't ready to answer questions. She considered calling Colin at The Gallery to apologize, then decided against that as well. It was best that their break had been complete. If they parted on good terms, he might be tempted to get in touch with her from time to time. Cassidy knew she could never bear the casual friendliness.

She packed up the dress she had worn on her flight from the studio. Her fingers lingered on the material as she placed it back in the dress box. So much had happened since she had first put it on. Quickly she smoothed the tissue over it and closed the lid. That part of her life was over. Turning, she went to the phone to call The Gallery. The clerk who answered referred her immediately to Gail.

"Why, hello, Cassidy. Where did you run off to?"

"I have the dress from the portrait and the key to the studio," Cassidy told her. "I'd like someone to come pick them up."

"I see." There was a brief hesitation before Gail continued. "I'm afraid we're just terribly busy right now, dear. I know Colin particularly wanted that dress. Be sweet and drop it by? You can just let yourself into the studio and leave everything there. Colin's away, and we're just swamped."

"I'd rather not —"

"Thank you, darling. I must run." The phone clicked. With a quick oath of annoyance, Cassidy hung up.

Colin's away, she thought as she picked up the dress box. Now's the time to finish it completely.

A short time later Cassidy pushed open the back door of Colin's studio. The familiar scents reached out and brought him vividly to her mind. Resolutely she pushed him away. Now is not the time, she told herself and walked briskly to his worktable to set down the dress and key.

For a moment she stood in the room's center and looked about her. She had spent hours there, days. Every detail was already etched with clarity on her memory. Yet she wanted to see it all again. A part of her was afraid she would forget something, something small and insignificant and vital. It surprised her that the portrait still stood on the easel. Forgetting her promise to leave quickly, Cassidy walked over to study it one last time.

How could he look at that, she wondered as she gazed into her own eyes, and believe the things I said? I can only be grateful that he did. I can only be grateful he believed what I said rather than what he saw. Reaching out a hand, she touched the painted violets.

When the door of the studio opened, Cassidy jerked her hand from the painting and whirled. Her heart flew to her throat.

"Cassidy?" Vince strolled into the room with a wide smile. "What a surprise." In seconds, her hands were enveloped by his.

"Hello." Her voice was a trifle unsteady, but she managed to smile at him.

He heard the breathlessness in her voice and saw there was little color in her face.

"Did you know Colin has been looking for you?"

"No." She felt a moment's panic and glanced at the door. "No, I didn't. I've been away, I've been working. I just . . ." She drew her hands away and clasped them together as she heard herself ramble. "I just brought back the dress I wore for the portrait."

Vince's dark eyes became shrewd. "Were you hiding, madonna?"

"No." Cassidy turned and walked to a window. "No, of course not, I was working." She saw the sparrow, busily feeding three babies with gaping mouths. "I didn't realize you were going to be in America this long." Say anything, she told herself, but don't think until you're out of here.

"I have stayed a bit longer in order to convince Colin to sell me a painting he was reluctant to part with."

Cassidy gripped the windowsill tightly. *You knew he would sell it.* You knew from the beginning all that would be left would be dollars and cents. Did you expect him to keep it and think of you? Shaking her head, she made a quiet sound of despair.

"Cassidy." Vince's hand pressed lightly on her shoulder.

"I shouldn't have come here," she whispered, shaking her head again. "I should've known better." She started to flee, but he tightened his grip and turned her to face him. As he studied her, he lifted a hand to brush her cheek. "Please . . ." She closed her eyes. "Please don't be kind to me. I'm not as strong as I thought I was."

"And you love him very much."

Cassidy's eyes flew open. "No, it's only that I —"

"Madonna." Vince stopped her with a finger to her lips. There was a wealth of understanding in his eyes. "I've seen the portrait. It speaks louder than your words."

Lowering her head, Cassidy pressed the heel of her hand between her brows. "I don't want to . . . I'm trying so very hard not to. I have to go," she said quickly.

"Cassidy." Vince held her shoulders. His voice was gentle. "You must see him . . . speak to him."

"I can't." She placed her hands on his chest, shaking her head in desperation. "Please, don't tell him. Please, just take the portrait and let it be over." Her voice broke, and when she found herself cradled against Vince's chest she made no protest. "I always knew it was going to be over." She closed her eyes on the tears, but allowed herself to be held until the need to release them faded. He stroked her hair and kept silent until he felt her breathing steady. Gently he kissed the top of her head then tilted her face to his.

"Cassidy, Colin is my friend —"

"Interesting." Cassidy's eyes darted to the doorway . . . and to Colin. "I'd thought so myself." His voice was quiet. "It appears I've been mistaken about more than one person recently." Even before he crossed the room, Cassidy felt the danger. "Gail told me I'd find you up here," he said when he stood directly in front of them. "With my *friend*."

"Colin . . ." Vince began, only to be cut off with a fierce look.

"Take your hands off her, and keep out of this. When I've finished, you can pick up where you left off."

Hearing the fury in his words, Cassidy nudged out of Vince's hold. "Please," she murmured, not wanting to cause any trouble between them. "Leave us alone for a moment." When Vince's hand stayed on her arm, she turned her eyes to him. "Please," she repeated.

Reluctantly Vince dropped his hand. "Very well, *cara*." He turned briefly to Colin. "I've never known you to be mistaken about anyone, my friend." He walked across the room then closed the door quietly behind him. Cassidy waited an extra moment before she spoke.

"I came to return the dress and the key." She moistened her lips when he only stared down at her. "Gail told me you were away."

"How convenient the studio was available for you and Vince."

"Colin, don't."

"Setting yourself up as a duchess?" he asked coldly. "I should warn you, Vince is known for his generosity, but not his constancy." His eyes raked her face. "Still, a woman like you should do very well for herself in a week or two."

"That's beneath you, Colin." She turned and took a step away, but he grabbed a handful of her hair. With a small sound of surprise and pain, she stared up at him.

His eyes were shadowed and dark, as was his chin with at least a day's growth of beard. It occurred to her suddenly that he looked exhausted. Thinking back, she knew he had never shown fatigue after hours of painting. His fingers tightened in her hair.

"Colin." In defense, she lifted a hand to his.

"Such innocence," he said softly. "Such

innocence. You're a clever woman, Cassidy."
His hands came to her shoulders, quickly,
ruthlessly. She stared up at him in silence,
tasting fear. "It's one thing to lie with
words, but another to lie with a look, to lie
with the eyes day after day. That takes a
special kind of cheat."

"No." She shook her head as his words
brought back the tears she had stemmed.
"No, Colin, please." She wanted to tell
him she had never lied to him, but she
couldn't. She had lied the very last time
they had been together. She could only
shake her head and helplessly let the tears
come.

"What is it you want from me?" he demanded. His voice became more infuriated
as tears slipped down her cheeks. The sun
fell through the skylight and set them
glinting. "Do you want me to forget that I
looked at you day after day and saw something that was never there?"

"I gave you what you wanted." Tears became sobs and she struggled against him.
"Please, let me go now. I gave you what
you wanted. It's finished."

"You gave me a shell, a mask. Isn't that
what you told me?" He pulled her closer,
forcing her head back until she looked at
him. "The rest was my imagination. Fin-

ished, Cass? How can something be finished when it never was?" His hand went
back to her hair as she tried to lower her
head. "You said that I'd drained you. Have
you any idea what these past weeks have
done to me?" He shook her, and her sobs
grew wilder.

"You were right when you told me that
painting was nothing more than your face
and body. There's no warmth in you. I created the woman in that painting."

"Please, Colin. Enough." She pressed
her hands over her ears to shut out his
words.

"Do you cringe from the truth,
Cassidy?" He tore her hands away, forcing
her face back to his again. "Only you and I
will know the painting's a lie, that the
woman there doesn't exist. We served each
other's needs after all, didn't we?" He
pushed her aside with a whispered oath.
"Get out."

Freed, Cassidy ran blindly for escape.

Chapter 10

It was late afternoon when Cassidy approached her apartment building. She had walked for a long time after her tears had dried. The city had been jammed with people, and she had sought the crowd while remaining separate. The pain had become numbed with fatigue. She was two blocks from home when the rain started, but she didn't increase her pace. It was cool and soft.

Inside her building she began an automatic search for her mailbox key. Her movements were mechanical, but she forced herself to perform the routine task. She would not crawl into a hole of despair. She would function. She would survive. These things she had promised herself during the long afternoon walk.

With the key at last in the lock, Cassidy lifted the cover on the narrow slot and pulled out her mail. She riffled through the advertisements and bills automatically as she started for the stairs. Her feet came to an abrupt halt as she spotted the return address on one of the envelopes. *New York.*

For several minutes she merely studied it, turning it over then back again. Walking back to her mailbox, she pushed the rest of her mail back inside then leaned against the wall. A rejection slip? she reflected, nibbling her bottom lip. Then where was the manuscript? She turned the envelope over again and swallowed.

"Oh, the devil with it," she muttered and ripped it open. She read the letter twice in absolute silence. "Oh, why now?" she asked and hated herself for weeping again. "I'm not ready for it now." She forced back the tears and shook her head. "No, it's the perfect time," she corrected then made herself read the letter again. There couldn't be a better time.

She stuffed the letter into her pocket and ran back into the rain. In ten minutes she was banging on Jeff's door.

Guitar in hand, he pulled open the door. "Cassidy, you're back! Where've you been? We were ready to call out the marines." Stopping, he took his eyes from the top of her head to her feet. "Hey . . . you're drenched."

"I am not drenched," Cassidy corrected as she dripped on the hall floor. She hoisted up a bottle of champagne. "I'm much too extraordinary to be drenched.

I've been accepted into the annals of literature. I shall be copywritten and printed and posted in your public library."

"You sold your book!" Jeff let out a whoop and hugged her. His guitar pressed into her back.

Laughing, Cassidy pulled away. "Is that any way to express such a momentous occurrence? Peasant." She pushed back her sopping hair with her free hand. "However, I'm a superior person, and will share my bottle of champagne with you in my parlor. No dinner jacket required." Turning, she walked to her own door, pushed it open then gestured. Grinning, Jeff set down his guitar and followed her.

"Here," he said after he had closed the door and taken the bottle from her. "I'll open it, you go get a towel and dry off or else you'll die of pneumonia before the first copy hits the stands."

When she came back from the bathroom wrapped in a terry-cloth robe and rubbing a towel over her hair, Jeff was just releasing the cork. Champagne squirted out in a jet.

"It's good for the carpet," he claimed and poured. "I could only find jelly glasses."

"My crystal's been smashed," Cassidy told him as she picked up her glass. "To a very wise man," she said solemnly.

"Who?" Jeff raised his glass.

"My publisher," she announced, then grinned and drank. "An excellent year," she mused, gazing critically into the glass. The wine fizzed gently.

"What year is it?" Jeff lifted the bottle curiously.

"This one." Cassidy laughed and drank again. "I only buy new champagne."

They drank again then Jeff leaned over and kissed her. "Congratulations, babe." He pulled the damp towel from her shoulders. "How does it feel?"

"I don't know." She threw her head back and closed her eyes. "I feel like someone else." Quickly she filled her glass again. She knew she had to keep moving, had to keep talking. She couldn't think seriously about what she had won that day or she would remember what she had lost. "I should've bought two bottles," she said, spinning a circle. "This is definitely a two-bottle occasion." She drank, feeling the wine rise to her head. "The last time I had champagne . . ." Cassidy stopped, remembering, then shook her head. Jeff eyed her in puzzlement. "No, no." She gestured with her hand as if to wipe the thought away. "I had champagne at Barbara

Seabright's wedding in Sausalito. One of the ushers propositioned me in the cloak-room."

Jeff laughed and took another sip. A knock sounded. Cassidy called out, "Come in, there's enough for —" Her words were cut off as Colin opened the door.

Cassidy's color drained slowly. Her eyes darkened. Jeff looked quickly from one to the other, then set down his glass.

"Well, I gotta be going. Thanks for the champagne, babe. We'll talk later."

"No, Jeff," Cassidy began. "You don't have to —"

"I've got a gig," he announced, lifting her restraining hand from his arm. She saw him exchange one long look with Colin before he slipped through the door.

"Cass." Colin stepped forward.

"Colin, please go." Shutting her eyes, she pressed her fingers between her brows. There was a pressure in her chest and behind her lids. Don't cry. Don't cry, she ordered herself.

"I know I haven't any right to be here." There was a low harshness in his tone. "I know I haven't the right to ask you to listen to me. I'm asking anyway."

"There isn't anything to say." Cassidy forced herself to stand straight and face

191

him. "I don't want you here," she said flatly.

He flinched. "I understand, Cassidy, but I feel you have a right to an apology . . . an explanation."

Her hands were clenched, and slowly she spread her fingers and stared down at them. "I appreciate the offer, Colin, but it isn't necessary. Now . . ." She lifted her eyes to his. "If that's all . . ."

"Oh, Cass, for pity's sake, show more mercy than I did. At least let me apologize before you shut me out of your life."

Unable to respond, Cassidy merely stared at him. He stooped to pick up the bottle of champagne. "I seem to have interrupted a celebration." He set the bottle back and looked at her. "Yours?"

"Yes." Cassidy swallowed and tried to speak lightly. "Yes, mine. My manuscript was accepted for publication. I had a letter today."

"Cass." He moved toward her, lifting a hand to touch her cheek.

Cassidy stiffened and took a quick step back. Catching the look that crossed his face, she knew she had hurt him. Colin slowly dropped his hand.

"I'm sorry," Cassidy began.

"Don't be." His voice had a quiet, final

quality. "I can hardly expect you to welcome my touch. I hurt you." He paused, looking down at his hand a moment before bringing his gaze back to her face. His eyes searched hers. "Because I know you as well as I know myself, I'm aware of how badly I hurt you. I have to live with that. I haven't the right to ask you to forgive me, but I'll ask you to hear me out."

"All right, Colin, I'm listening," Cassidy said wearily. She drew a deep breath and tried to speak calmly. "Why don't you sit down."

He shook his head and, turning, moved back to the window and looked out, resting his hands in the sill. "The rain's stopped and there's fog. I still remember how you looked that night, standing in the fog looking up at the sky. I thought you were a mirage." He murmured the last sentence, as if to himself. "I had an image in my mind of a woman. My own idea of perfection, a balance of qualities. When I saw you, I knew I had found her. I had to paint you."

For a moment he lapsed into silence, brooding out at the gloom. "After we'd started, I found everything in you I'd ever looked for — goodness, spirit, intelligence, strength, passion. The longer I painted you, the more you fascinated me. I told you once you bewitched me; I almost believe it. I've never known a woman I've wanted more than I've wanted you."

He turned then and faced her. The play of the light threw his features into shadows. "Each time I touched you, I wanted more. I didn't make love to you that night on the houseboat because I wouldn't have you think of yourself as just one of my lovers. I couldn't take advantage of your being in love with me."

At his words, Cassidy's eyes closed. She made a soft sound of despair.

"Please, don't turn away. Let me finish. The day the painting was finished, you denied everything. You said the things I'd seen had been in my own imagination. You were so cool and dispassionate. You very nearly destroyed me. . . . I had no idea anyone had such power over me," he continued softly. "It was a revelation, and it hurt a great deal. I wanted more from you, I needed more, but you told me you had nothing left. I was angry when you ran away, and I let you go. When I came here later, you were gone.

"I've been out of my mind for over two weeks, not knowing where you were or when — worse, *if* — you were coming back. Your friend next door had your cryptic little note and nothing else."

"You saw Jeff?" she asked.

"Cassidy, don't you understand? You disappeared. The last time I saw you, you were running away from me, and then you were gone. I didn't know where you were, or how to find you, if something had happened to you. I've been going slowly mad."

She took a step toward him. "Colin, I'm sorry. I had no idea you'd be concerned. . . ."

"*Concerned?*" he repeated. "I was frantic! Two weeks, Cassidy. Two weeks without a word. Do you know what a helpless feeling it is to simply have to wait? Not to know. I've haunted Fisherman's Wharf, been everywhere in the city. Where in heaven's name were you?" he demanded furiously then held up a hand before she could answer. She watched him take a deep breath before turning away from her. "I'm sorry. I haven't had much sleep lately, and I'm not completely in control."

His movements became restless again. He stopped and lifted Cassidy's discarded glass of champagne. Thoughtfully, he studied the etchings on the side. "An interesting concept in a wineglass," he murmured. Turning back, he toasted her. "To you, Cass. To only you." He drank then set down the empty glass.

Cassidy dropped her eyes. "Colin, I am sorry you were worried. I was working, and —"

"Don't." The word stopped her, and her eyes shot back to his. "Don't explain to me," he said in more controlled tones. "Just listen. When I walked into the studio today and saw you with Vince, something snapped. I can give you excuses — pressure, exhaustion, madness, take your pick. None of them make up for the things I said to you." His eyes were eloquent on hers. "I despise myself for making you cry. I hated the things I said to you even as I said them. Finding you there, with Vince, after looking for you everywhere for days . . ." He stopped, shaking his head, then moved back to the window.

"Gail arranged the timing very well," he said. "She knew what I'd been through the past two weeks and knows me well enough to predict how I'd react finding you alone with Vince. She sent him up to the studio on a fictitious errand before I got back to The Gallery. She told me the two of you were meeting up there. She made the suggestion, but I grabbed on to it with both hands." He rubbed his fingers over the back of his neck as if to release some tension.

"We'd been occasional lovers up until about a year ago when things got a bit complicated. I should have remembered whom I was dealing with, but I wasn't thinking too clearly. Gail's decided to take a long — perhaps permanent — sabbatical on the East Coast." He paused a moment then turned to study her. "I'd like to think you could understand why I behaved so abominably."

In the silence Cassidy could just hear Jeff's guitar through the thin walls of the apartment. "Colin." Her eyes searched his face then softened. "You look so tired."

His expression altered, and for a moment she thought he would cross to her. He stood still, however, keeping the distance between them. "I don't know when I fell in love with you. Perhaps it was that first night in the fog. Perhaps it was when you first wore that dress. Perhaps it was years before I met you. I suppose it doesn't matter when."

Cassidy stared at him, robbed of speech. "I'm not an easy man, Cassidy, you told me that once."

"Yes," she managed. "I remember."

"I'm selfish and given to temper and

black moods. I have little patience except with my work. I can promise to hurt you, to infuriate you, to be unreasonable and impatient, but no one will love you more. No one." He paused, but still she could only stare at him, transfixed. "I'm asking you to forget what makes sense and be my wife and my lover and mother my children. I'm asking that you share your life with me, taking me as I am." He paused again, and his voice softened. "I love you, Cass. This time, my destiny's in your hands."

She watched him as he spoke, heard the cadence of his native land grow stronger in his speech. Still he made no move toward her, but stood across the room with shadows playing over his face. Cassidy remembered how he had looked when she had flinched away from his touch.

Slowly she walked to him. Reaching up, she circled his neck with her arms then buried her face against his shoulder. "Hold me." His arms came gently around her as his cheek lowered to the top of her head. "Hold me, Sullivan," she ordered again, pressing hard against him. She turned her head until her mouth found his.

His arms drew tight around her, and she murmured in pleasure at their strength. "I love you," she whispered as their lips parted then clung again. "I've needed to tell you for so long."

"You told me every time you looked at me." Colin buried his face in her hair. "I refused to believe I'd fallen in love with you, that it could have happened so quickly, so effortlessly. The painting was nearly finished when I admitted to myself I'd never be able to live without you."

His voice lowered, and he drew her closer. "I've been crazy these last two weeks, staring at your portrait and not knowing where you were or if I'd ever see you again."

"Now you have me," she murmured, making no objection when his hands slipped under the terry cloth to roam her skin. "And Vince will have the portrait."

"No, I told you once some things can't be sold. The portrait has too much of both of us in it." He shook his head, breathing in the rain-fresh fragrance of her hair. "Not even for Vince."

"But I thought . . ." She realized that she had only assumed Vince had been speaking of her portrait. There was a new wealth of happiness in the knowledge that Colin had not intended to sell what was to her a revelation of their love.

"What did you think?"

"No, it's nothing." She pressed her lips against his neck. "I love you." Her mouth roamed slowly up his jawline, savoring what she knew now was hers.

"Cass." She felt his heart thud desperately against hers as his fingers tightened in her hair. "Do you know what you do to me?"

"Show me," she whispered against his ear.

With a groan, Colin kissed her again. She could taste his need for her and wondered at the strength of it. Her answer was to offer everything.

"We'll get married quickly," Colin murmured then took her lips again, urgently. Inside her robe, his hands ran in one long stroke down her sides, then roamed to her back to bring her closer. "Very quickly."

"Yes." Cassidy closed her eyes in contentment as his cheek rested against hers. "I already have the perfect dress." She sighed and nestled against him. "What will you title the painting, Colin?"

"I've already titled it." He smiled into her eyes. *Sullivan's Woman.*